CW00518540

DIRTY BOSS

LP LOVELL

Alex,

The destroyer...

LP Lovell

Copyright © 2016 LP Lovell.

All rights reserved.

No part of this book may be reproduced in any form or by any electronic or mechanical means, including information storage and retrieval systems, without written permission from the author, except for the use of brief quotations in a book review.

Cover Designer: Pretty In Ink Creations

Editor: Stevie J. Cole

❀ Created with Vellum

PROLOGUE

LONDON'S square mile is witness to a revolution, a new breed of business woman. We out-earn, out-work and out-play our male counterparts. We work the system, play the game and most importantly, win. In a city full of sharks only the most ruthless make it to the top of the pool.

No matter how much money I make, or how successful I am, I am and always will be a woman in a mans word. Employers will tell you they support equal rights. On paper it seems that way, but I know better. It has fuck all to do with rights and more to do with the fact that men are men, and they will always see women as something to stick their dick in. Unless you play the game. Unless you win. And in order to do so, rules must be followed.

Rule number one: Never, ever, fuck the boss.

Rule number two: As an extension of rule one, never let the boss hit on you. The second the boss hits on you, you're done. Reject him and you're the bitch who turned him down. Fuck him, and you're the office slut that he cheated on his wife with. Either way, you're screwed and I guarantee, that the next round of redundancies, you're out.

Rule number three: Anybody might be somebody. Be careful what you say, what you do and most importantly, who you fuck. That annoying twat who's drunkenly dragging his eyes all over your tits...he might be your next boss or the guy you need to cut a deal with next week, hell, he could be a client. Always err on the side of caution and no matter how much you want to tell someone to fuck off, don't.

Rule number four: Always appear beyond reproach. A male colleague can go out, get pissed and turn up to work smelling of whiskey and looking like he got run over. That's fine. The boss will probably laugh it off and give him a manly pat on the back. The same does not apply to a woman. Keep it clean, keep it legal and most importantly, keep it private.

Rule number five: Play nice. I may be painfully aware of the inadequacies of my male colleagues at times, but I cannot point that out. I must be one of the guys, yet unattainable in every way. This is the only way to earn their respect, and that will be a factor when it comes to the next promotion.

This is what it takes to be a tiger shark. I pay the price willingly. Because one day, I'll be the CEO.

1

"FUCKING SHIT." I whisper, scanning the graphs on the computer screen. I press the intercom in front of me. "Jonathan get in here."

The door opens and my assistant shuffles through the door nervously smoothing his hands down the front of his shirt. "Ms. Roberts." He stammers.

"Are these figures right?" I ask, turning the screen towards him and pointing at the print. For the most part the boy is a stuttering mess, but he's a statistical genius. He glances at the screen and then drops his eyes to the floor.

"Yes, um, they're this morning's reports."

"I'm aware of that. What I'm asking is whether that can possibly be right?!" I snap, jabbing my finger against the glass at the point where one of my biggest client's stocks just took a twenty percent dive. Variations I can deal with. Stocks move up and down all the time. Every day, every hour, but twenty fucking percent...

"Um, yes. I believe so."

"Shit. Get Samson on the phone. Tell him I'm on my way

up." I push up from my desk and stride from the room, slamming the door behind me.

The office is quiet at this time of morning. I'm always here an hour before anyone else in order to have a head start on any shit hitting the fan.

The only person I see is one of my colleagues, Dan, otherwise known as the competition. He's a slimy prick who spends most of his time balls deep in the latest secretary. "Georgia." He starts.

"No time." I say, walking straight past him.

"I heard NewTec just went down!" He shouts after me, a smug edge in his voice. I ignore him and keep walking.

I cross my arms and tap the toe of my shoe against the floor as I wait for the lift to climb to the top floor of the building. My heart is pounding, adrenaline spiking through my veins. I live for the rush of making money, but I hate losing. At anything.

The lift pings and the doors slide open revealing the enormous lobby, the walls adorned with some crappy art which my boss, Collins, seems to think makes him cultured. Two mahogany desks sit on either side of the lobby, stationed by the pretty secretaries he likes to keep. The one on the right eyes me, pouting her bright pink lips.

"He's in a meeting..." She says, but her voice trails off as I storm past her and shove the double doors to his conference room open.

Collins and two other men are sat at his monstrosity of a conference table. He never has a meeting with more than three people so I have no idea why he has it. I guess it saves him having to whip his dick out. The room smells of strong coffee and pastries. All three men look up at me as I walk in, their conversation halting. Martin Collins is a wiry, short man in his forties. He got where he is by being a shady fuck, but he's extremely successful and makes a lot of money, so I don't judge his methods. After all, he has everything I want.

"Georgia." He says, before his features morph into a scowl. "I'm in the middle of—"

"This can't wait."

He opens his mouth to object and I cock an eyebrow at him. "Uh, gentleman, give me a minute would you? I'm so sorry." I say, putting as much sugary sweetness in my tone as possible. They both smile and nod. Collins gestures for me to step through the door that leads to his adjoining office. He shuts the door and turns to face me, a scowl on his face.

"What are you doing?" He snaps.

"Twenty percent!" I say, slamming the print out on his desk. He frowns, examining the papers.

Giles Samson has been my client since the beginning. You shouldn't have favourites, but he's mine. He took a chance on a young stock broker, and within a year I had turned a fifteen percent profit for him. He owns a twenty percent share in NewTec. The only one with a bigger stake is Arnold Montes, the company founder, with a twenty-five percent stake. Arnold is Collins' client and he is fucking me in the arse. The only way stock drops that quickly is when someone starts unloading shares. A lot of bloody shares.

"You tell Montes that if he keeps selling, I will drop his fucking shares at twenty percent cost, and I'll squeeze those saggy balls of his until he squeals like the rat he is." Giles would agree to it, because like me, he hates losing and he refuses to be fucked like a cheap whore. I'd see Giles lose money before I watch Montes make some by screwing us over.

Collins sighs and pinches the bridge of his nose as he leans against his desk. "Montes is one of our top—"

I snatch the papers from his hand and lock eyes with him. "Save the shit, *boss*." I snarl. "Fix it, or I will."

I'm usually controlled, calm, collected. I have perfected the façade which is necessary to thrive as a woman in the dog eat dog world of business by being a pit bull in sheep's clothing. Every so often though, something like this happens, my temper gets the best of me and I bare my teeth.

This is the precarious line Collins and I walk. He pays my salary. He's my boss and I'm his employee. My temper tantrums should be enough to get me fired, but here's the cincher, he needs me far more than I need him. Good stock brokers are hard to find, and if I walk out of here, I'll take at least ten major clients with me. I have him by the short and curlies. If my clients are happy, I'm happy. They make millions and I make my six figure yearly bonus. He fucks me over, and I'll ram the figurative cock so far up his arse, he'll feel it in the back of his throat.

Call it a mutual respect if you will, an understanding that we both have. And as long as I don't undermine him in front of anyone else, he'll take it like the money hungry little bitch he is. I walk out of his office and straight through the conference room without sparing him or his companions a second glance.

2

It seems that Collins managed to pull his finger out of his arse and fix the shit with Montes. I've never had to get on the phone and tell a client that they've lost money. And I don't intend to because I don't lose. Ever.

At seven I switch off my computer and leave the office, pressing the call button for the lift. When the doors open I squeeze in amongst the suit-clad businessman for whom city life has dramatically dampened their sense of personal space.

On the next floor one of the guys from accounting gets in, cracking a smile when he sees me. "Georgia. You at Ice later?" He says, stepping close enough that I can smell the coffee on his breath.

I flash him a small smile. "Of course. Where else am I going to get a decent Martini around here?" His smile widens and his eyes drop to my chest.

"Great." He winks at me. Brilliant.

Rule number Five: Play nice. You might not like someone, or in this case, even know who the hell they are, but always be tactful. Men will often be over familiar, because their dick would disown them if they didn't at least chance it. There's a fine line between putting your foot down and being called a bitch, ice queen or whatever else they come up with. You must become one of the boys, unattainable but not ostracized. When I came to this city I thought being good at the job would be enough, oh, how wrong I was. London is a giant chess board, a game in which strategies, deception and rules define your success.

"I'll see you there." He says as the lift pings, the doors opening into the lobby. Everyone but me and a couple of older guys get out. I press the button for the underground parking garage.

It's true that it would be faster to get the tube home rather than sit in the bumper to bumper London traffic, but I work hard for my money, so forgive me if I'd rather sit in my Mercedes than an underground train pressed up against god knows who. No thank you.

I slide behind the wheel and pull into the crawling London traffic.

Ice is one of the most exclusive bars in London. It's forty-two floors up, overlooking the twinkling lights of London's square mile sprawled below. The lift doors open, and as always, the room is packed with suit-clad bankers, all drinking and laughing as they wind down from their stressful day jobs. I can't even see the bar through the wall of bodies.

"Hello, boys." I say, flashing a smile at the group I know well as fellow stock brokers at Elite. They part like the red sea, allowing me to make my way to the bar. I put just a little more sway in my hips as I push through them. I don't miss the way eyes trail over my body, lingering just a little too long. Several colleagues greet me, and at this stage in the night it's with an air of respect. Of course, once they've bought a few glasses of over-priced whiskey that will change.

Quinn is propped on a stool at the bar, her legs crossed elegantly. She's wearing a pencil skirt and a sleeveless emerald green silk blouse that's just one button shy of risqué territory. Some guy in a suit is attempting to talk to her, but she's shut him down, barely even acknowledging his presence. She flicks her long, dark hair over her shoulder, a look of utter disdain painting her features as she purses her blood red lips.

I stride up to her and her face breaks into a fake as fuck smile, as though she's never been happier to see me. She stands. "So good to see you, babe." She says as she throws her arms around my neck. "Oh my god. I want to stab him." She hisses in my ear.

Quinn is my best friend. They say it's lonely at the top, and they aren't lying. Women like us don't have time for bullshit and niceties, everything is about the win. But London is a work hard, play hard city. A girl always needs someone to play with. Quinn and I are, and always have been, cut from the same cloth. We met in University right here in London and have supported each other through the highs and lows that is life in the city.

She unwinds her arms from around me and sits back down. I turn to the guy still lingering, leaning on the bar and propping his foot on the rung of the bar stool next to Quinn.

"Excuse me." I say, placing my hand on the stool and waiting for him to move. A sly grin pulls at his lips as his gaze crawls over my body. His eyes eventually lock with mine. I stare him down, my expression icy as I watch the smile slowly slip from his lips.

He removes his foot and straightens, brushing his hands down the front of his suit. As soon as he does so, I smile at him. "Thank you so much." I say, false nicety lacing my voice.

Blinking, he starts to say something, but I turn my back on him and take a seat, facing Quinn. Rule number three: No matter how much you want to tell someone to fuck off, don't. In this city, everybody might be a somebody, and anybody could have the power to ruin you. This game is as much about diplomacy as anything else. You can be a bitch, but just make sure you're above reproach when you do it.

Quinn gives a small nod, indicating that he's left.

"Thanks." She says as she makes eye contact with the bartender. He turns away to start on making our martinis. We come here way too much. "I was struggling to get out of that one." She rolls her eyes. It's the difficult line we walk, constantly rebuking our male co-workers whilst still remaining 'friends' with them. I would never, ever, fuck anyone in or around the office. This bar is a hub of bankers. Sleep with one and you might as well have fucked them all. Either way, your integrity is compromised and without that you don't have shit.

The bartender places the martini in front of me and I take a sip. Quinn pays the man and he leaves.

"So, how is Mayers?" I ask Quinn. She works for Mayers and Co., a corporate law firm.

"Same shit, different day." She shrugs. There is one area where Quinn and I differ massively. I won't be happy until I'm the CEO. That's the dream, the grand plan. For Quinn she just wants to make enough money that she can leave this city, buy a bar on a beach somewhere and never look back. I don't blame her. There are times when I'd love nothing more than a beach and my own company, but we do what we must, and the truth is I'd be bored after a day. I live for the rush of making money, for the thrill of the big city. I love the game far too much to ever leave it.

A few guys I know from the office stand in a group at the bar behind us. A couple of them veer away, focusing their attention on us.

"Georgia, I hear you saved the day." One of them says as he moves in front of me. I can't remember his name, but I know he's a broker. Maybe Nate? He looks like a Nate. He has a glass of whiskey in one hand, while the other is shoved into the pocket of his trousers, pushing his open jacket back and drawing the eye to what I know is a platinum Rolex on his wrist. His blond hair is swept back, the front rebelling into a small quip.

Each of the brokers have a list of clients and many of us share an investment. I may have a client with a twenty percent stake in a company, and quip boy here might have a client with a two percent stake in the same company. But they can guarantee that if my clients have a stake then I'll put my own damn money in before I let that stake drop. I guess he was sweating when he saw the drop this morning.

I cock an eyebrow. "Of course."

"Well, that deserves a drink. Let me buy you one." I want to roll my eyes but I don't.

Smiling, I slowly shake my head. "I have one." I gesture to the Martini in front of me. "Any more and I'll be positively drunk."

Him and his friend talk to us for a while, until we're interrupted by the steadily growing volume of the guys behind us, their voices getting louder the more they drink. I pretend not to hear the crass comments about who's going to fuck the new secretary first.

I glance at Quinn and give a small jerk of my chin. Time to extricate ourselves. "Well boys, we need to get going."

"Oh, come on. Stay for one more drink." Quip boy says, a charming smile lighting his face.

"My yoga class is at six." Quinn says. "We don't look this good by sheer fluke you know." She says with a wink before sliding off her stool.

They step aside and we move past them, managing to make it to the lift with only a couple more interruptions.

I hail a cab outside the bar and we slide into the back. Now the fun really begins.

Rule number four: Be above reproach, and keep it private. I like to keep my social life separate from the prying eyes of other bankers, the sharks just waiting for a hint of blood in the water. In this city a woman must appear squeaky clean, beyond recompense, beyond judgment. As far as they know, we've gone home to get our beauty sleep. Little do they know.

3

FRIDAY NIGHT and I'm having to spend my time at this shit.

Elite is having its annual charity party bullshit in which people gather and pretend to like each other, even though they'd all rather be doing other things. The lucky few will have managed to come up with an excuse, but for the most part we have to come or face being on the boss' shit list. On the up side, the drinks are free. I'd love to neck twelve martinis, but there are clients here and of course, the rules.

Giles Samson, one of my oldest clients has turned up with his mail order bride. Giles may be the client I've made the most money for, but in a world obsessed with what someone can do for another, he's also a friend.

His wife is clinging to his arm with a face like a slapped arse. She's an ex-super model who gave it up for him apparently. I'm pretty sure most Eastern European girls would give up their left tit to marry a guy as wealthy as Giles, plus he's only in his forties, and he's not a bad looking guy. The entire notion of a gold digger makes me laugh and cringe at the same time. Still... he's getting to plough a twenty five-year old pussy every night, and she's driving around in a Bentley. Everyone's a winner. No judgment here.

A waiter passes by and I grab a glass of champagne off the tray before I make my way over to him. Giles is pretty much the only person I actually want to talk to here.

His face breaks into a wide grin when he see's me. "Georgia!" He beams, his perfectly white teeth gleaming against his tanned skin. Giles kind of looks like the baddy in a bond film. He's originally from Norway and his hair is so blonde it's almost white. He even has the matching eyebrows and really pale blue eyes that seem to look straight through you. He still speaks with a slight accent and laughs a lot. Basically he looks, sounds and acts like a crazy rich dude, which would be accurate.

"Giles." I say, a genuine smile pulling at my lips.

He shrugs away from the grasp of his wife and wraps me in a bear hug. I used to find him a bit strange and definitely unprofessional, but I've come to realize that it's just how he is. I like that he doesn't give a shit about social etiquette.

"You look lovely." He says, the laughter lines creasing the corners of his eyes.

I roll my eyes. "You always say that."

"Well, it must be true then." He chuckles, his wife glaring at me the entire time, or maybe that's just her resting face? I can't tell.

I take a deep breath and plaster a smile on my face as I turn to face her. No matter how little time you have for wives and girlfriends, you have to make an effort. Women are naturally threatened by a woman who not only has more in common with her man but also garners his genuine respect, add in attractive and they want to claw my eyes out. Men like to pretend they wear the trousers but everyone knows that behind every powerful man is a woman pulling his strings. If she's not happy then he's not happy.

I turn towards, Erika? Shit, I think that's her name. I really need to work on that.

"Hello. I don't think we've officially met. I'm Georgia." I say, holding my hand out to her.

She eyes my outstretched hand. "Erika." She shakes my hand tentatively.

"I'm sorry I missed the wedding, I had pressing business in New York." I tell her, bullshitting for all I'm worth. Giles invited me to his wedding, but as much as I like Giles, I try not to blur the lines between business and friendship *that* much.

She nods and turns away, making her way to the bar. Giles chuckles, drawing my attention back to him. "What?"

He shakes his head. "I appreciate the effort, I really do, but she's somewhat prickly." He says, holding his hands out like a bad impression of Edward scissorhands. I shake my head, suppressing a laugh.

"She's beautiful."

"The beautiful ones are always crazy." He says, his accent caressing the words. "I know this and yet, I have a weakness." He shrugs.

I laugh. At least he's honest.

We talk business for a few minutes before I decide I had best do a quick recky of the party so I can bail. I have somewhere I need to be.

I end up talking to some guys in expensive suits, because when it comes to networking, always aim for the guys with the money. If I'm going to have to spend my time at these events, then it needs to be worthwhile. I've got as far as ascertaining that they're American and that the younger guy likes tits when Collins sidles up beside me, wrapping an arm around my shoulders. I go rigid, the contact instantly putting me on edge.

"I see you've met Georgia. She's one of our best. If you like money, then she's your girl." He laughs to himself. So apparently they're here as clients or potential clients. My boss sways on his feet slightly, leaning against me. God, I hate being touched.

"She seems very...capable." The pervy one says. I have to try very hard not to glare at him.

"You're too kind." I say. Fuck me. "I should go and talk to Giles before he leaves, but it was lovely to meet you." I say with so much sweetness in my voice I'm almost making myself vomit.

I slip from Collins' grasp and move away from the small group. I'm done. I'm going. I slip into the bathroom to touch up my make-up before I make a break for it.

I'm rummaging through my clutch bag in search of my lipstick when I hear the door open, close, and then I hear the ominous sound of a lock clicking into place. I look up from my clutch and into the mirror to find Collins behind me, leaning against the door. Oh, this not good. Not fucking good at all.

I spin to face him, crossing my arms over my chest. "You know this is the women's bathroom, right?" I keep my tone light and joking.

A creepy smirk pulls at his lips as he pushes away from the door and drags a hand through his greying hair. "Oh, I know." *Fuck, fuck, fuck.*

He moves towards me slowly and I start side stepping, trying to maneuver around him in the small space, but it's impossible. He steps close, too close. I can smell the stench of whiskey on his breath.

"You're so beautiful, Georgia." *Code fucking red!*

I laugh lightly. "If it's flattery you're going for then you might want to aim it at Dan, his ego is much more receptive."

He reaches up and brushes a strand of hair away from my cheek. I flinch away from his touch, praying that he'll drop this shit. My shoulders are so tense they're starting to ache. I hold my breath, waiting, hoping that he'll stop, but when he closes his eyes and leans into me I know it's game over. I duck out from my position between him and the vanity, causing him to stagger forward and bump against the sink.

I stride towards the door, flicking the lock off and yanking it open. "Expect my resignation on your desk Monday morning." I throw over my shoulder before I exit the room.

Fucking Collins, stupid prick. I know he's drunk and in the morning he might regret this, but he crossed the line. The rules are simple and are there for a reason. Is it my fault he hit on me? Of course not. Should he be expected to keep control of his dick? Hell yes! But that's not the way it works. I can bitch, moan and whine about it, or accept that there will be consequences. I just won't be hanging around for them.

4

I TAKE a sip of my chai latte, needing the caffeine badly this morning.

Giles sits across from me in his immaculate pinstripe suit with his elbows braced on the table, his chin propped on his clasped hands. We meet every other Monday for breakfast, always have for as long as I can remember. It's this personal touch that makes me like Giles so much. This morning is more than just a casual breakfast meeting though. His pale blue eyes watch me carefully as I word what I need to say in my head. I've worked with him for years, and yet, the way he scrutinises everything always has me feeling inadequate in some way.

"You look troubled, Georgia." He says in that accent of his, making each word sound almost lyrical.

I put my coffee down and lean forward slightly, meeting his eyes. "I'm leaving Elite." I say.

His brows drop into a ghost of a frown before he nods slowly. "Why?"

I would never tell anyone else the real reason why, but I consider Giles friend. A good friend. Despite my efforts to keep things between us professional, he's almost fatherly towards me. "Collins hit on me, and we both know how that goes."

He sighs heavily. "I wondered how long it would be. He looks at you like..." He waves his hand around. "Like you are the golden fleece."

I snort. "I just thought I would let you know. I totally understand if you still want to broker with them. They're a very reputable firm."

A small smile pulls at his lips and then he chuckles lightly. "My dear girl, my loyalty is not easily bought, but for you it is unfailing." I'd be loyal if someone made me as much money as I make him. But I know it's more than that. He has always believed in me.

I met Giles at a cocktail party. I'd attended it to network, but of course most of London's upper cut just saw me as something pretty, except Giles. He always says that he saw a fire in me. He's a little crazy I guess, but then the ridiculously rich always are. Now I manage fifteen million pounds worth of stock for him. The thought of Collins' face when he realizes that his drunken play has cost him one of his biggest clients makes me smile.

"Have you thought of going out on your own?" He asks.

I shake my head, clasping the coffee cup between my hands. "I'm not ready."

He cocks his head to the side, narrowing his eyes at me in contemplation. "You're the best damn broker I've ever known."

"Well," I laugh. "I appreciate the vote of confidence, but I'm going to go for another bank."

"Okay." He shrugs. "I'll put the word out. As soon as the big guns hear that Georgia Roberts is up for grabs you'll be inundated with offers."

I hope he's right.

When I get to work I don't even go to my office. I take the elevator straight up to the top floor. The lift doors slide open and I step out. Only one secretary is in at this hour. She nods, waving me through.

I walk straight through the conference room and stop outside the heavy wooden doors that lead to Collins' office. Taking a deep breath, I steel myself before I push the handle down, shove the door open, and walk into his office with my head held high. Collins is sat with his elbow propped on the desk and his hand covering his eyes.

He slowly looks up, watching me as I approach him. I place my written resignation on the enormous desk, sliding it front of him.

"What's this?" He asks, his brow furrowing as his eyes trace over the letter.

"I told you I would have my resignation on your desk Monday morning." I say, keeping my voice level.

His eyes meet mine. "Georgia, I...I'm sorry. I was drunk. Let's just forget about it. Please." There's a begging tone to his voice.

"Thank you for the opportunities you've given me in my time here. That resignation is for a thirty-day notice, however, given the circumstances I feel it would be best if it was effective immediately." He looks as though he may argue, but then I see the resignation in his eyes.

He drags a hand over his face, scrubbing at the slight stubble coating his chin. Now that I look at him properly he looks worn, troubled. "Samson?" He asks.

So that's what has him so stressed. I guess I'd be stressed having to bring that news to the board of directors.

"You'll have to ask him." I fight a smirk. "Goodbye, Martin." I turn on my heel and stride out of his office without a backward glance.

I've worked for Elite Finance for five years. I've clawed my way from an intern to one of the best stock brokers here. As daunting as it is stepping away from the known, the unknown is exciting. There are always jobs and opportunities for someone with my skills, after all, making money never goes out of fashion.

I clean out my desk and leave the office. I can feel people's eyes on me as I carry the small box of belongings to the lift. No one says anything, but I know what they're thinking. There are very few reasons for instant dismissal, what with all the employment rights. There's only really one...stock fraud. Seeing as Collins is unlikely to admit the real reason, the speculation will run rife. I've never given a shit about the opinions of others though. I'm not about to start now.

I drive home and pull my car into the space outside my Thames side apartment. When I reach my front door, there's a large manila envelope propped against it. Balancing my box of belongings on my knee, I crouch awkwardly and swipe the envelope off the floor. I unlock the door and drop the box in the hallway, shoving it against the wall with my foot.

I go straight to the kitchen, grab the orange juice from the fridge and pour out a glass. Once in the living room, I take a seat on the couch, placing my glass on the coffee table. I rest the envelope on my thighs and study my name in elegant hand writing across the front of it. I have no idea who it's from.

I tear open the top and pull out the wad of papers from inside. The paper itself is thick, expensive. Across the top is a gold foil logo with scripted writing through it: Banks and Redford.

The covering letter is addressed to me and offering me a job. Not an interview. Not a meeting. A job. Banks and Redford are an investment manager in Mayfair, no, they're *the* name in investment. I've heard that they head hunt talent from across the globe. Their success rate is second to none, and they only take on clients with a minimum five-million investment. And they're offering *me* a job.

I place the letter face down on the coffee table and skim read over the first page of an employment contract, my eyes stopping on the six figure salary and signing bonus stamped in bold black letters on the crisp crème paper. I drop the papers onto the table and chew on my bottom lip as I think. This can't be right, surely? If something seems too good to be true, then it usually is.

5

I DUMP my gym bag in the corner of the room and roll out my yoga mat next to Quinn's before I lie down and start stretching. Morning sun spills through the tall windows that line the yoga studio, casting a redish tinge through the room with the sun rise.

"I was worried you'd died." Quinn says as I pull my knee into my chest.

"No, I just stayed home last night."

"So, as good as then. I heard you got sacked for fraud." She says, a smile playing over her lips. Quinn knows all about Collins' sloppy Friday night play. When I told her she looked at me as I'd just been sentenced to death.

"Wow." I roll my eyes. "That didn't take long."

"How did Collins take it? I would pay good money to have seen the look on his face."

"Okay, I mean, what could he say? He has no one to blame but himself and his fucking dick."

She stretches her legs out in front of her and folds her body forward, reaching for her toes. "What's the plan now?"

I pull my arm across my chest, holding it in place with the other. "I have a job offer."

"Fuck me, you work fast. Who with?"

"I got home yesterday to find a written offer on my doorstep. It's with Banks and Redford."

Her eyes widen and she blows a strand of hair out of her face. "Seriously?" I nod. "You kept that quiet. When did you interview with them?"

I cock an eyebrow. "I didn't." She frowns. "It's shady if you ask me."

She rolls her eyes. "You think everything is shady. Have you ever thought that maybe you're just good at what you do?"

I snort. "Oh, I know I'm good, and they might even have heard it, but that fast? What are they? James Bond?"

She smiles, sitting up and bracing her hands behind her. "Don't look a gift horse in the mouth, George." She says, shaking her head. "You've been offered a job with one of the best firms in London. I hear the guy who owns it is set to make the Forbes list this year."

I take a deep breath. "We'll see."

I walk into Mayfair House at seven forty-five. The steady clip of my Louboutins echoes around the vast marble lobby, making the woman at the desk look up. Her eyes are bright and her hair and make-up flawless.

"I'm here to see Mr. Redford." I tell her. "Georgia Roberts."

She taps a few buttons on her keyboard and then smiles politely at me. "Take elevator number four. It will take you straight to the top floor."

Even the lift looks expensive, with gold veined marble on the floor, and immaculate mirrors on the walls and ceiling. There are no buttons on the wall, only the small screen showing the climbing numbers as we rise.

A fissure of nervous energy has me tapping my foot against the floor. Angus Redford and Landon Banks founded Banks and Redford ten years ago, and in a short space of time they have dominated the market and carved out their own legacy. Google is your friend and all that. That kind of success takes a certain type of man though, and I won't pretend I'm not a little intimidated by the prospect of having to prove myself to someone like that.

I tried to research the two of them on a personal level. It seems that Angus runs the company, whereas Landon seems to spend his time managing his many other businesses all around the world. From bars to transport companies to clothing lines—the guy seems to be into everything. I guess he's more of a silent partner

The lift doors open on the top floor. Despite the fluttering in my stomach I force myself to walk with purpose. I step into what doesn't even feel like a room. The floor under my feet is marble, but the walls are made entirely of glass, with the exception of the wall directly opposite me, which houses the double doors that I guess lead to the main office. In the middle of the space is another secretary sat at a desk.

"Miss Roberts." The middle aged woman greets me, moving out from behind her desk and stopping in front of me.

"Yes." I respond.

She flashes me a wide genuine smile. "I'll just let him know you're here." I stand there while she picks up the phone, muttering a few words before hanging up.

"He's ready for you." She says, moving around the desk

and leading me to the doors. "Don't look so nervous dear. He doesn't bite." She laughs and knocks on the door once before pushing it open.

"Miss Roberts for you, sir." She opens the door wider, allowing me to step inside. Oh wow. This room is amazing, the glass walls meeting in a V shape, giving the office a panoramic view of London. It's pretty impressive.

I focus on the man sat in front of me. At the back of the room are two massive desks, but closer to the door is a coffee table with two sofas either side facing each other. It's here that he sits, his elbows propped on his knees as he studies a piece of paper on the coffee table in front of him.

He slowly rises to his feet, dragging his eyes away from his reading. He buttons his suit jacket as he approaches, his long legs eating up the space between us. I don't know how I expected Angus Redford to look. I guess, old, with a paunch. I know he's in his early forties, and the streaks of grey at his temples give that away, but other than that he looks barely a notch over thirty.

He holds his hand out to me, a warm smile on his face. "Ms. Roberts. I'm Angus Redford." He introduces himself, the slightest hint of a Scottish accent in his voice.

"It's nice to meet you." I say, shaking his hand. His blue eyes are sincere as he smiles, the lines around his eyes sinking into his face from what looks like years of laughter. Some people have the ability to put you at ease with a look. Angus Redford is one of those people.

"Come. Sit." He resumes his position on the sofa, turning the piece of paper he was reading over. I sit opposite him, crossing one leg over the other and resting my hands on my knee

"You have a beautiful office." I comment.

He laughs. "Over the top isn't it? Landon likes 'space', he

says it helps him think. It took me about a month just to get over the vertigo every time I came in here."

I smile at the sound of his deep laughter booming around the room. He picks up a jug of water that's on the coffee table and pours himself a glass before pouring another and pushing it in front of me. He leans back and props his ankle on his knee, picking some lint off his trouser leg. I can see a flash of pink and green stripey socks and I try not to laugh. "Now, I'm sure you have some questions Ms. Roberts."

"I'll admit that this all seems rather mysterious."

"Yes, sorry about that. Long story short, Giles is a good friend of mine." I pause, scraping my teeth over my bottom lip. I adore Giles, but he's always put an undeserved amount of faith in me. He's probably made me out to be some sort of bloody gold mine. I know I'm good, but these guys don't want good, they want exceptional. And no matter how much confidence I might have, I think anyone would struggle to have that much faith in their own ability. Especially in a business where luck has as much to do with success as anything else. "He's very good with numbers and an extremely good judge of character." He continues, lifting his glass of water to his lips and taking a sip. "He says you're the best there is."

I take a deep breath. "Giles has been very supportive of my career. I'm grateful to him. He's a very loyal client."

A small smile pulls at his lips. "And one that would follow you wherever you go." Finally. I hate not knowing the ulterior motives behind a persons actions, because without that you're blind. But there it is, the real reason they've offered me a job. Business is all about what one person can do for another and I have no doubt that my skills are in demand, but not unique. Giles though, my portfolio, the revenue I can command...that's something any investment firm worth their salt would want.

"As I said, he's very loyal."

He claps his hands together and stands up. "Excellent. Well then I see no need to discuss any further. You have the proposed contract. If you're happy with it then you're welcome to start tomorrow."

He stands and holds his hand out to me. I climb to my feet and shake it, not entirely sure what I'm shaking on, but I guess I have a new job.

"Something tells me you and I can make a lot of money together." He says, a grin spreading over his face.

6

I'VE BEEN at Banks and Redford for two weeks, and I'm killing it. I thought when I walked in here that I'd probably be working fourteen hour days and reaching for impossible figures with a list of fifty clients. That's not the case at all. I managed to bring fifteen clients with me from Elite, totalling twenty-five million pound's worth of existing investments. Those are my clients, that's it. I really wish I could have seen Collins' face when he realised that his dick lost him that much money. Needless to say, Angus is pleased. He wants me to meet him for drinks tonight and introduce me to the ever illusive Landon Banks. Apparently he's in London for a few weeks. Angus and I have a good dynamic going, he knows which side his bread is buttered and that I make him good money. As long as I do that and he keeps the bonuses coming, we're good. Banks has very little to do with the company and therefore my life, so I don't see our meeting as anything more than a formality.

I have to admit though, I'm curious. Information is hard to come by when it comes to Landon Banks. A Google search brings up a list of his companies as well as a few images of him at various charity benefits. Not that that means shit. The rich and powerful must always keep up appearances by donating to the latest fashionable charity.

The whispers around the office suggest that Banks is a cut throat businessman, but popular with the ladies. I had to listen to one of the secretaries this morning simpering over how amazing he is. I just about managed to keep a straight face in front of her and not roll my eyes. I've seen images, and I won't deny he's a good looking guy. He looks like something out of GQ magazine. But he's my boss, which is an instant turn off. I might as well be into pussy for all the effect he'll have on me. I'm a professional. Once someone is off the table, they're off the table, and in this city, that's pretty much everyone I meet.

The cab draws to a stop outside Rouge and I hand the driver some money before climbing out. I pull my coat tighter around me as a cool breeze whips across my face.

As soon as I step inside I spot Angus leaning against the bar, laughing with the girl serving him. Over the last couple of weeks I've noticed that there's something about Angus Redford that's very different to the usual banker types. There's an easiness to his demeanour that I rarely see in men with his kind of power. He smiles easily and doesn't take himself too seriously.

He turns to face me as I approach, a wide smile on his face. "Georgia! The woman of the moment." He leans in and kisses my cheek. "What can I get you to drink?"

"A martini please." I glance around the bar as he orders. It's exactly what you expect of London bars. Clean, modern, bare.

He takes the drinks from the stainless steel bar and moves over to a table in the corner of the room. I slide my coat off and sit down.

"You look lovely, Georgia." I fight the smile trying to make its way onto my face. If I could describe Angus in one word it would be cute, the guy that every girl friend zones when she should really marry him. "Landon will be here at some point, though he's rarely on time for anything social. A business meeting and he's there fifteen minutes early, social occasion and he avoids it like the plague."

"Oh?" I pick up my drink and take a sip.

"Don't take it personally. He's a funny bastard." He shrugs one shoulder and I don't ask him to elaborate.

"How long have you two known each other?" I ask.

He drags a hand through his curly hair and leans back against the seat. "We weren't unlike you and Samson. I was his broker. He had a lot of money and I made him more." He picks up his glass, swilling the whiskey around. "I'd never met him in person until one day he invited me to a meeting with him, away from the bank." He smiles as his eyes focus on a spot on the table. "He just put it all on the table, no bullshit. He thought the bank was fucking him over, and he wanted a private broker. Offered to double my wage and have me handle all his investments, so I did. Of course, then his friends wanted me and his friend's friends. He worked out that he could take a cut from it and before you know it we were official brokers."

"So you work for him?"

His eyes lift to mine. "No, he offered me a fifty-fifty stake as soon as we got big enough to need offices." He frowns slightly. "Some might say it's because he doesn't want to run it, but I'll tell you this, Georgia, I've never come across a fairer man than Landon Banks."

Well, now I'm *really* intrigued.

"Hmm, a nice guy whose also successful. Rare."

He chuckles. "I'm not sure 'nice' is the first word I'd use

to describe him. Landon is...an anomaly. You'll see what I mean."

I pick up my drink and open my mouth to respond when something shifts in the air. A slight hush falls over the room. My skin prickles with awareness. I pause with my glass halfway to my lips, and glance over my shoulder. People try to maintain their conversations, but every eye has subtly shifted to the man standing in the doorway. He moves through the room, easily parting the crowd without saying a word.

When I first came to this city I thought that all the 'suits' looked the same. But the longer you stay here the easier it is to see the differences between a two-grand watch and a twenty-grand watch, a thousand-pound suit and a ten-thousand-pound suit. And this guy is wearing a fifty-grand Rolex and a silk suit that I wouldn't even like to put a value on. The navy material fits him perfectly, clinging to his narrow hips and broad shoulders. The way he moves is almost graceful, but every single fibre of his being bristles with power. So much so that he seems to suck all the oxygen out of the room. His dark hair falls slightly over his forehead. He looks like he literally woke up and dragged his hand through it. He has a face that belongs on a runway in Milan, and a jawline that would make Brad Pitt envious. But honestly, his draw isn't in his looks, his body, or even the fact that I can practically smell the money on him- It's the power that surrounds him like an aura. He lives and breathes it as though it's a part of him and he were born to wield it. I can't decide whether I'm un-nerved by him or in awe of him. Both I think.

I can't look away from him as he approaches the table. He narrows his eyes at me before slowly flicking them over my body in a way that's nothing short of pure righteousness, as though he has a right to everything that I am. Hell, maybe he does. I feel like he just stripped me naked and exposed me in the worst kind of way. The way he looks at me it's like he can see every weakness, every desire, every sordid secret. I don't even know the man and yet he's unhinging me with each passing second. Heat creeps up my neck and into my cheeks. As quickly as it started, it stops. He flicks his eyes away, quickly dismissing me before he lowers himself into the seat next to Angus, unbuttoning his jacket with a deft flick of his wrist. I slowly release the breath I was holding and focus my gaze on Angus. No man has ever done that to me. Ever. I clench my fists beneath my table until my nails bite into my palm, the sharp pain clearing the last of the foggy haze he seems to have my mind in.

"The wanderer returns." Angus says with his usual easy smile.

A waitress bustles over, placing a glass of whiskey in front of my boss—the new one—the hot one. He picks it up and takes a sip, and even the way he does that has me clenching my thighs together. The way he holds the glass, his throat working as he swallows. Jesus. Why am I fucking looking? Do *not* look at him.

"Dubai was getting too hot." He says, his lips slightly pulling up at one corner.

Angus leans forward, gesturing towards me. "Well, Georgia Roberts, meet Landon Banks, my business partner."

Banks turns his attention on me, his eyes colliding with mine. I'm ready for him this time. "A pleasure." He says, his deep voice caressing the word elegantly.

"It's nice to meet you, Mr. Banks." Still his eyes hold mine, even as he lifts the glass of whiskey to his lips and takes a sip. I steel myself and refuse to look away. Because I'm Georgia Roberts and the day I bow to a man is the day

I'm fucking done, even if he is my boss. The air suddenly feels heavy with an unspoken challenge, the weight of it pressing in on me. Something passes between us, like two predators sizing each other up, and even though I know I'm out-leagued, I stand my ground, refusing to admit defeat. A lamb baring its teeth at a lion. Not many men can inspire an instant respect from me, but this one does. A very healthy respect.

"Ah, Giles is here." Angus says, bursting the weird bubble that Landon has me in. I turn my gaze in the direction of the door, and still I can feel Landon's eyes on the side of my face.

Giles approaches the table and shakes hands with Angus. "Angus." He smiles before repeating the gesture with Landon. Then he turns to me, his face breaking into a wide grin. "Georgia." Giles and I have an odd relationship that just steps the other side of professional. I've never thought much of it before, until now, with Landon Banks studying me like prey. I stand up and Giles kisses my cheek. "Looking as glamourous as ever my dear."

I laugh. "Well, you got me a job with these guys. I had to up my game."

He scoffs as he takes the seat next to me. "Don't listen to her. She always makes me feel positively shabby, though not my bank account." He laughs in that infectious way of his and I find myself laughing with him.

I glance across the table at Landon and find him watching me stoically, his head tilted slightly. I don't do nervous or flustered, or even self-conscious, but this guy has me feeling all of the above. And I hate it.

Angus gestures the bar maid over, and she places a glass in front of Giles, leaving an entire bottle of whiskey this time. Giles pours himself a glass.

"A toast." Angus says, lifting his glass. "To Georgia."

I roll my eyes. "To money." I correct, focusing my attention on Angus and Giles so as to avoid Landon's intense gaze. Until we clink glasses that is, at which point I accidentally neck my entire martini. Giles and Angus don't seem to notice, but Landon's attention is fixed firmly on me and his lips pull into just a hint of a smirk, amusement flashing in his eyes. I glare at him, which makes the ghost of a smile turn into a real one. I've decided I don't like him.

My phone rings in my bag, and I take it out, glancing at the screen. *Quinn.* I almost want to sigh in relief. I must thank that girl for having incredible timing.

"Will you excuse me, gentleman? This is important."

Giles and Angus nod offering an 'of course', while Landon says nothing. I stand and make my way to the hallway by the bathrooms.

When I call Quinn back she picks up on the first ring. "Hey. What are you up to?" She asks.

"Meeting the other boss, the Banks in Banks and Redford." I should take this as an opportunity to leave, go and meet Quinn and stay away. Landon is not a guy I need to spend any amount of time around. He has me flustered, because honestly, if he weren't my boss, if I didn't have my rules, he's exactly the kind of guy I would fuck. The simple fact that I'm attracted to him is reason enough to give him a very wide berth.

"Oh, what's he like?"

"Uh, hard to say at this stage."

"Okay. Well message me if you get done early." She says.

"Sure."

"Have fun!" She offers as a parting.

I hang up and tuck my phone inside my clutch before heading back into the small bar. When I approach the table

Giles is animatedly telling one of his stories, and Angus is laughing. Landon is...looking bored.

"I think I'm going to call it a night."

Giles checks his watch and shakes his head. "I thought these young ones were supposed to be able to party all night and still make it into the office by eight." He says to Angus.

"You're not supposed to encourage such things Giles." I smile.

He stands up, and kisses my cheek. "Fine. Breakfast. Monday?"

"Of course."

"We'll have a meeting tomorrow, Georgia." Angus adds. He glances at his glass of whiskey, frowning slightly. "Best make it at ten." He grins.

I smile. "I'll be there." I turn on my heel when that deep voice halts me.

"I'll walk you out." Landon's deep voice halts me.

I take a deep breath and turn to face him, a smile plastered on my face. "That's kind of you, but unnecessary." I say through my gritted teeth.

He stands and falls into step beside me with barely a goodbye to Giles or Angus. "I'm leaving anyway." He explains, fastening his jacket as he walks, smoothing his hand over his matching navy tie. He looks like he just stepped right out of the pages of a magazine. Perfect, unruffled, completely in control of everything around him.

The silence seems to reign between us as we get in the lift, and once inside it's as though that invisible power of his beats away at me, effecting me in ways that it shouldn't. It's a strange mix of exciting and infuriating. I force myself to stand as far away from him as possible, pressing my bare arm against the mirrored wall.

He shoves his hands in his trouser pockets, fixing his

gaze on the floor. "Angus likes you." He says, almost to himself.

"You sound surprised."

"He rarely takes such a personal interest in an employee." He drags his eyes over me again as though trying to work me out.

"I'm good at what I do, Mr. Banks. I make money." I say a little too abruptly.

He narrows his eyes. "So I hear."

The lift comes to a stop and the doors glide open silently. He maintains his position beside me as I stride across the lobby.

London hums with life as I step outside, pausing at the top of the steps, trying to spot a taxi. I know there's a taxi rank around the corner.

"It was nice to meet you, Mr. Banks." I hold my hand out to him.

He eyes it, cocking an eyebrow and making me feel self-conscious, as though simply shaking his hand is some awkward event.

I lower it and he steps close to me, taking my hand and lifting it. He dips, and my breath seizes in my lungs when his lips brush over my knuckles. He lingers just a little too long and I allow it, standing there numbly with my pulse hammering in my ears like an idiot. I snatch my hand away, tucking it behind me, but I swear I can still feel where his lips have imprinted on my skin.

"A pleasure, Miss Roberts." He says, a distinctly calculating look in his eyes.

Without another word I turn away from him, heading down the street in search of a taxi.

"You're walking home?" He calls after me. I turn back to face him.

"These are five hundred pound shoes." His expression remains blank and this time I do roll my eyes. "Taxi." I say as way of explanation.

He sighs and steps up to the black car lingering at the curb, opening the back door wide and stepping to the side. "Get in."

"Honestly, I'm fine with a taxi, but thank you." I argue.

His eyes lock with mine and he flashes me a look that brooks no argument. "Get in the car, Georgia." There's just a hint of a growl in his voice, and when he says my name, it makes me shiver. The fact that he just ordered me to get in the car, coupled with the fact that he effects me has my hackles rising fast. My temper over rides rational thought and I find myself stepping closer to him until we're toe to toe. I tilt my head back, meeting his dark gaze.

"Sorry, *boss*, I don't take instructions well outside of the office, and uh, stranger danger and all that." His eyes spark with something dark and dangerous and I find myself being drawn towards him. I catch myself and stagger back a step. "See you soon." I say, flashing him a blinding smile before turning on my heel and walking away. I have somewhere I need to be and no one, not even Landon Banks is going to keep me from going.

I grab a taxi and head into Mayfair, the heart of London's secretive and elite social circle. This is the part of my life that no one knows about, the sordid and beautifully dark underbelly of the city's wealthy upper class. In this city, everyone knows someone and everyone talks. People like me, we're obsessive. It's what makes us so good at what we do. But that obsession often leaves a person open to many vices. The places that I go after dark, they feed every conceivable vice in every possible way.

7

Masque is where all manner of creatures come to play, to fulfil warped desires without judgement or persecution. After all, you can't judge what you can't see.

I slip the mask out of my handbag and tie the ribbons at the back of my head, pinning them into my hair with some grips. I knock on the door of what looks like a respectable and extremely expensive town house in the centre of London's most affluent area. The door opens, revealing a guy in a black suit, a plain black mask covering his eyes. He glances at my membership card and he waves me through.

Inside it looks exactly how you'd expect a high end sex club to look. Dark, luxurious, sensual. Rock music fills the room, contrasting wildly with the velvet chaise lounges and crystal chandeliers. Within the club, people resume a new identity. Their masks *become* their identity. Mine looks like a cat, the faint stripes of a tiger painted along the delicate lines that outline my face and accentuate my sharp cheekbones. There's a certain thrill in hiding, because in hiding who I am, it allows me to be who I *really* am. I come here for one reason, to be liberated on every level.

I go to the bar and perch on a stool, crossing my legs and allowing my short black dress to ride up my thigh. The waiter slides a martini in front of me and I thank him. I allow my gaze to drift around the room, shopping, because everyone in here is on the menu. My gaze stops on a guy sitting on one of the sofas, his fingers buried in the pussy of the woman straddling him. His mask is distinctive, made of white porcelain and depicting a Greek god. I know from experience that he has a body like a god as well. Sometimes I like to be surprised by a new partner, but other times I like to know that I'm going to be satisfied. Apollo, as I call him, always satisfies my more aggressive appetites, and tonight I feeling positively savage after my interaction with Banks. There's nothing like a powerful man to make my inner alpha bitch rear her head with bared teeth.

I down the martini and stand, swaying my hips a little as I make my way to Apollo. He looks up, his eyes meeting mine through the mask that covers his eyes and nose. His lips kick up slightly on one side as he assesses me with a cockiness I've come to expect of him. The woman moans, her fingers clinging to his shoulders and scratching over the material of his open shirt.

"Come." I say to him.

"Well, it would be rude not to finish the lady." He says, humour lacing his voice.

I tilt my head to the side and study the girl, her long blonde hair cascades down her bare back as she throws her head back. I step close to her and grab a handful of her hair, fisting it. She moans, pushing her chest out. He watches me intensely as his bicep tenses, his fingers sinking deeper inside her.

I bend over, dropping my face into the crook of her neck and placing a kiss to her soft skin before sweeping my tongue up the side of her throat. Her breath hitches and she trembles gently. I lift my eyes to meet his, and I see the spark of lust in them, the need eating away at him as I wrench her head back even further and slide my free hand down her chest, pinching her nipple between my thumb and index finger. She bucks and writhes, moaning as she rides his hand.

"Fuck." He says, completely enraptured by the sight of her coming apart under our combined touch. When she's done, he practically throws her off him and rises to his feet. My eyes instantly hone in on the bulge straining against the material of his trousers. His shirt remains open, the hard planes of his stomach on display. I jerk my head towards the stairs and he follows me without question.

This house has twenty rooms, each one identical to the other. For those who like their play a little rougher, there's the basement which houses a dungeon. I have certain tastes, but they don't venture into 'chain me up and beat me' territory.

We pass a line of doors, all with a red ribbon tied on the door. These are the occupied rooms, although some people don't bother with the ribbon in the hope that someone walks in on them. To each their own. Then of course there are those who like to be openly watched, like that girl, they just fuck in one of the many public rooms downstairs.

I push open the door to a vacant room and step inside, watching him close it behind him with a resounding click. The room is simple, a four poster bed, chaise lounge, racks of toys and instruments on the far wall, and an attached bathroom.

I back away until my legs bump the chaise. Apollo slides his shirt over his shoulders, allowing it to fall to the floor as he stalks towards me. He's is a good looking guy, and utterly shameless. He likes sex any way he can get it. If it makes him come, he's game. The harder the better. Any means necessary. And that is what makes him so appealing.

I reach behind me and lower the zip on my dress, shrugging out of it.

Of course with that mask, I can't clearly make out his expression as I bare my naked body to him. It makes him seem hard and implacable. For some reason it makes me think of Landon. It shouldn't be a turn on but it is.

I step out of the dress at my feet and hook my thumbs into my underwear. I pause for a second, call it dramatic effect if you like, before slowly sliding them down my legs. Still he doesn't make a move or breathe a sound. I'm left wearing nothing but my Louboutins.

Lowering myself onto the chaise lounge behind me, I smile and beckon him forward with a crook of my finger. He obliges, stripping out of his remaining clothes as he crosses the room and stops in front of me. I trail my fingers down his stomach to his hard dick just inches from my face. I'll suck dick like a pro when the feeling strikes me, but right now, it doesn't.

"Get on your knees." I command, and he does, dropping to the plush carpet, completely naked.

I trail my fingers over my thighs and spread my legs open. Wide open. His gaze falls to my pussy, his eyes flashing along with the rapid rise and fall of his chest.

"Kiss me."

He doesn't hesitate as he grips my thighs with both hands. Hot breath hits my pussy before his lips do, brushing gently across my clit. My nails rake into the unforgiving material of the chaise as his tongue lashes me. This is why I pick him. No questions, no bullshit. Just pleasure and compliance.

He works his tongue over me until I'm trembling, lingering on that beautiful precipice and just waiting to go tumbling off the edge. When I break, it's perfect, powerful, the orgasm rolling over me like a rogue wave. Aftershocks ripple through my torso as I lean my head against the back of the chaise, trying to catch my breath. I close my eyes, a small smile on my lips, because that was good, but what's about to come is even better. Sex is about physical and mental satisfaction, and I like to release in every way before I leave this club.

My eyes flash open as I drag myself upright. His hands are still on my thighs and my orgasm is all over his lips. I push to my feet but he doesn't move. I go to my discarded handbag and take out my favourite toy, also fondly known as The Destroyer. I clip the harness in place around my hips and yank the straps tight—don't want it slipping now. Then I pick a lube from the shelf . This club is nothing if not accommodating. I pick up one called Sex Water, the slogan written on the bottle reads; 'for when spit and courage isn't enough'.

Apollo glances over his shoulder, watching as I move toward him with the big purple cock jutting out in front of me.

He smirks. "You could at least suck a guy's dick first."

I rake my fingers through his short hair. "You know I make you come harder with a cock in your arse."

"True." The thing about coming to a sex club is that all the taboos that are unacceptable outside this room, are completely acceptable inside it. Apollo likes a fake dick in his arse. He likes me to fuck him. He gets off on it, and me? I get to plough the fuck out of a guy. I get to own him and make him my bitch for the small amount of time that I'm in here with him. Trust me, to a girl who is constantly bowing and scraping to men inside the office, fucking him is empowering, freeing even.

"Stand up and bend over, legs spread." I order

He does as I say, grabbing the back of the chaise lounge firmly. His cheeks spread and I get a view of his waxed balls and arsehole. I guess if you're into this kind of thing then you need to make sure the grass is cut.

I squirt a generous helping of lube on The Destroyer and grab his hips, lining up the purple cock before I push forward. The tip disappears inside him and the sight has me pressing my thighs together. I totally get why guys are obsessed with watching their dick slide inside a pussy. He drops his head forward, a ragged gasp leaving his lips as I push just a little more. When I feel him relax completely, I slam home until my thighs meet the backs of his. A choked groan fills the air as he tries to adjust.

"Take it." I tell him, my voice laced with warning.

Of course he's twice my size, and could tell me to fuck off easily, but he won't, because this is what he likes, and I give it to him.

I pull out and thrusting back in slowly. "Fuck." He hisses, muscles tensing and rolling beneath his skin. Then I grip his hips and I fuck him. Hard. The straps of the toy rub against my clit and a low moan escapes my lips. I fuck him until a thin sheen of sweat covers my body and he's pushing back against me, panting and groaning while he strokes over his cock furiously. I slow the pace, thrusting deeper, harder. He lets out a long guttural groan as every muscle tenses and then quivers violently. I keep going, so close to the edge of oblivion that I can practically taste it. The straps rub over my clit one more time, and my muscles clench as a bolt of pleasure rips through me. I fuck him until I can barely stand, until he's begging me to stop, slamming his hand on the back of the chaise like he's tapping out. His legs give way and he collapses to the floor, breathing heavily. His come is all over the chaise and the carpet.

"Look at the mess you made." Dropping to a crouch, I fist his hair and nip at his ear. "I think you should lick it up." And he does, licking his own come off the chaise. It shouldn't be as hot as it is.

By the time I've gone to the bathroom and cleaned up, Apollo is getting dressed. He looks a little worse for wear, but then he always does, and yet he always comes back for more the next week. I slip into my dress and straighten my mask before I stride out of the room without a backward glance.

This is what I do every Friday night. It's my release and at times my salvation. Hell, I'd even call it therapy. We all find different ways of coping with the stress of life, this is mine.

8

I SPEND the weekend hanging out with Quinn. We go for a run in Hyde park, binge watch Netflix and hit the city hard on Saturday night. It's a standard weekend.

Its Monday morning and I follow my usual routine, stopping on the way into the office and picking up an espresso. I'm always one of the first people into the office and when I step out of the lift on the thirty ninth floor it's quiet, dare I say peaceful as I make my way to my corner office. I close the door behind me and shrug out of my suit jacket, tossing it over the back of my chair. Every morning I go through the same routine. I print off my current stocks and shares and the rates and take them to Angus. It's an almost impossible task, but we try to stay ahead of the market as best we can.

I take the papers out of the printer and leave my office, taking the stairs to the floor above where Angus' office is.

His secretary is already there, the same as every morning. She smiles brightly at me but says nothing as I pass her. I knock once and open the door, focusing on the papers in my hand as I walk across the massive office.

"McClellan seems to have taken a dive this morning, but it'll pick back up by tomorrow. I think we should push for investments into Suntech. SolarX just went down, so there will be a market shift. I'll call…" I look up half way through my run down and realise that the figure sat at Angus' desk is not Angus. It's Landon. His dark hair is still damp as though he hasn't long been out of the shower. His suit is a charcoal grey today, but fits him every bit as well as the navy one. His eyes fix on mine as he leans back in his chair casually, twirling a silver pen between his fingers. He places his elbows on the arm rests, steepling his fingers in front of him as his eyes move subtly over my body. I swallow heavily as I feel the flush threatening to creep over my cheeks.

"How do you know McClellan will pick up tomorrow?" He asks.

It takes me a few seconds to remember what he's talking about. "Call it a feeling. Intuition. Experience, whatever you want."

He says nothing, and I fidget uncomfortably, shifting my weight from one leg to the other. His eyes track the movement. "And is that how you make decisions, Ms. Roberts? Intuition? Guess work?"

I cross my arms over my chest, and mimic his arsehole expression. "It's done me well so far. No one can predict the future."

His eyes narrow and his lips press into a flat line. In the heavy silence I can hear my own pulse hammering in my ears and it fucking shouldn't be. What is it about him? I'll admit that he intimidates me, but I'm Georgia Roberts, I don't get intimidated by anyone. The air seems to crackle between us and it makes me uncomfortable. He's my boss, except he's not. He's just a guy who owns part of the company and stops in every now and then. He leans forward and drops the pen on the desk, the metallic thud sounding far too loud in the silence.

"Angus will be in shortly. I'll tell him you wanted to speak with him." He says, tearing his eyes away from me and focusing on his computer screen.

"No need." I turn on my heel. "He trusts me to do my job." I throw over my shoulder as a parting blow. He says nothing as I leave the room, slamming the door a little too loudly behind me.

I've barely been in my office five minutes when there's a knock at the door. "Come in!" I shout.

The door opens and a tiny little red head in a skin tight black dress slips in, her shiny red heels sinking into the thick carpet as she walks up to my desk.

"I'm Eva." She says, sticking her hand out across my desk. I shake it.

"Um, Georgia. Why…"

She drops into the chair on the other side of my desk, crossing her legs and clasping her hands in her lap. "Oh, I know. I mean, it would be silly if I didn't even know the name of my new boss." She flashes me a perfect white smile.

"New boss?"

"Uh-huh. I'm your new assistant." She says brightly.

"Who I didn't hire." I add.

"Oh." She whispers, leaning forward as though to tell me some big secret. "Well, Julie downstairs got fired." She says quietly before silently mouthing 'under performance'. "So, you need an assistant. I need a boss. Here I am." She inspects her perfectly manicured fire engine red nails.

I'm not entirely sure what to make of her. She looks like

the kind of girl who got the job by blowing the boss, except I'm the boss, so...

"Okay. I mean, I don't really need an assistant..."

She rolls her eyes and jumps to her feet with a little hop. "Of course you do. Look at this place." She scoops the stacked papers off the corner of my desk and skims over the top one, moving over to the filing cabinet. Wordlessly she opens it and starts filing things away.

"Um, thanks." I say, frowning.

"You have an appointment in half an hour with Mr. Redford and a Ms. Wilkes, a new client." She says, whilst still filing the papers.

"I'm aware."

"I've organised to have lunch put on in the conference room for the meeting, and you should know that Ms. Wilkes is an avid campaigner for children's charities and spent six months in Africa helping children with Malaria. She's like a hippy who had really *really* rich parents." I frown at her back, and she eventually turns, focusing over her shoulder at me. "She's not a corporate chick, but pick the right companies and she'll invest."

I take it back, this girl might be helpful. "Thank you, Eva."

"No problem." She says, smiling wide before she walks to the door and pulls it open. "I'll move my things today. We're going to have so much fun." She squeals.

Okay, she might be good but any more of that girly squealing shit and we're going to have issues.

9

I BRACE my palm against my floor to ceiling office window, listening to my client have a meltdown on the other end of the phone.

"David." I sigh. "Stock goes up and yes, it goes down. It will go back up."

"I'm out by forty grand over night." He says, agitation in his voice. David Murdock is a relatively new investor. I took him on last year after I was recommended to him by another client of mine. He's new. New money and new to the game.

"That's stock for you. Tomorrow you could be up by forty grand. I told you when you signed with me, if you want safe, go and buy houses. The greatest risks are taken for greater reward and this is a marathon, not a sprint." He sighs heavily into the phone. "Just give it a week." I say.

"Fine. I'll give it a week. I guess I'll either win or lose big time."

"I don't lose Mr. Murdock." And with that I hang up the phone and drag a hand through my hair.

I turn away from the window and freeze when I spot a

figure standing in the door way. Landon. I bite back the sigh that wants to leave my lips.

"Landon. Do you need something?" I ask a little abrasively. Today has been a giant bag of shit and I really am not in the mood to deal with him.

A slow smile pulls at his lips. "I see where you get your reputation."

I ignore his comment and raise my eyebrows as I stare at him, waiting for him to voice the purpose of his visit.

"Walk with me." He says, jerking his head towards the hallway and turning around.

"I have work to do." I say to his back, shuffling some papers on my desk.

He goes very still before he glances back over his shoulder, his gaze crashing into mine. The hairs on the back of my neck stand on end and a small shiver works over my body. It's that feeling you get in the calm before a storm. "Walk with me." He repeats in that low gravelly voice, barely above a growl. It makes me want to punch him and strip naked at the same time.

I frown as I follow him out of my office. How does he do that? I catch Eva's eye as we pass her desk. She fans herself as I walk past and I roll my eyes. Landon strides through the hallways and people stare at him, watching him like he's some kind of Messiah. I'm pretty sure he thinks he's god.

He gets in the elevator and I stand there for moment, half wanting to turn and walk away, preferably while giving him the bird over my shoulder since he's summoned me like a dog with absolutely no explanation. The other half of me is mesmerised by everything that is him. He raises a brow questioningly as he steps forward, slamming his hand against the doorway to stop the doors closing.

"I don't have all day, Ms. Roberts."

I sigh and step into the lift beside him. He takes his phone out of his pocket, his fingers moving quickly over the screen. He barely spares me a glance and it allows me to study him, not because I want to appreciate him, but because I want to work out what it is about him above all other men that makes me *want* to stare at him, aside from the obvious.

His lips are set in a hard line as he studies the screen, narrowing his eyes slightly. Even now, standing across the lift from him with absolutely no contact or interaction, I'm on edge, my stomach clenching uncontrollably. It feels like a weight has settled on my chest, physically hindering my ability to breathe properly. His tongue darts over his bottom lip quickly and I wonder what his tongue would feel like on my skin. What the fuck? He's my boss.

The lift pings and as the doors slide open I almost breathe a sigh of relief. He steps out with that unhurried, calm demeanour of his, sliding his phone back into his jacket pocket as he moves.

He holds the door open for me and I expect him to get into the black town car waiting at the curb, but instead he starts walking down the street.

"Uh, where are we going?" I ask, hurrying after him.

"Lunch." He doesn't even look at me.

I have to jog every few strides to keep up with him. "I have a meeting in half an hour."

He ignores me and I stop. Fuck him. I'm not running after him because he's decided he doesn't want to look like a loner while he gets his lunch.

He takes a few steps before he whirls around with an exasperated sigh. "I moved your meeting to three o' clock. Any other objections?"

He moved my meeting? Okay, I just need to breathe. He's

the boss. He can move a meeting. He raises his brows, waiting. "Fine. I'll come as long as you stop running down the street. These shoes weren't made for walking," I snap.

He glances at my shoes before lifting his gaze back to my face. "No. They were not." It should be an innocent comment, but the way his eyes flash, the way his voice rumbles over the words has images of my Louboutins either side of his face flashing through my mind. He's. The. Boss.

"Are we going to stand on the pavement all day?" I storm past him without waiting for an answer. He falls into step beside me.

I hate being out of control. I like to predict everything, to know what is coming, and I did not predict Landon Banks. I knew he was wealthy and good looking, but of course, I didn't think it would even be a thing. The man is like crack to ovaries. I hate him. He's like a massive anomaly fucking with my perfectly balanced life.

We walk for about a mile, and in that time neither of us says a word to the other. He eventually stops at a small café, holding the door open and gesturing for me to walk ahead of him. I glance around the place with only a handful of tables and a list of specialities written in chalk on a board behind the counter. It's certainly not the sort of place I was expecting when he said he wanted to do lunch. He takes a seat at a small table near the window and I sit opposite him, hugging my handbag in my lap.

The waitress takes a drinks order and as she walks away, I can feel Landon's eyes burning into the side of my face, just like they were last night. "So, this is...nice." Since when did I stumble over small talk?

"I like the food here." He says simply. I'm starting to wonder if he's socially inept or just a man of few words.

The waitress comes back with our drinks after a few

minutes of awkward silence. She places them in front of us and then takes our order. I order a salad while Landon orders a burger. I find myself staring at his stomach where his suit clings to his muscular frame and wondering how the hell he gets away with eating a burger. The waitress scurries off, leaving me alone with Mr. Cryptic. He says nothing for long moments until the silence just leans into awkward territory.

"You brought me to lunch so you can stare at me?" I ask eventually.

"I like to understand the people who work for me, Ms. Roberts. I don't understand you. That is why I brought you here."

I"The only thing you need to understand, Mr. Banks is that I'm good at my job. Everything else is irrelevant."

He taps his index finger over his full bottom lip and my eyes track the movement. "Yes, you are." He muses. "But everything is relevant. I'm curious, why did you leave Elite Finance?"

I can't help but stiffen slightly. "I just needed to move on."

He drops his hand from his mouth and rests it on the table, rapping his knuckles on it. "Don't lie to me. It irritates me."

My temper fires up like the little red line on a thermometer that's been thrust into boiling water. I hate being questioned. I do my job, and I keep my private life private. End of. My eyes meet his, refusing to back away. "I don't care what does or does not irritate you." I say through gritted teeth. "Unless it pertains to my job, I wasn't aware that I need to disclose my life story."

His lips twitch and then he throws his head back and laughs. The grin looks so out of place on his normally serious face. "See, that right there." He points at me. "So professional, so *restrained*, and yet I can see what you really want to say written all over your face." I glare at him and he continues to watch me as if I'm a freak of nature. "I hear that you slept with Collins."

"You heard wrong." I say, disgust lacing my voice. "You've officially just put me off the idea of lunch."

"That bad?" He cocks a brow, that wry smile still on his face.

"Okay, I did not stick it to Collins. That is all you need to know."

He watches me for a few seconds before he shrugs and leans back in his chair. "Okay."

"Okay." I repeat.

"So, tell me, how did you becomes friends with Giles Samson?" He drags a hand through his perfect dark hair and his chest muscles flex with the movement. Damn him for looking like that. Damn me for noticing.

I drag my eyes away from his body and focus on his face. "I've known him for years. He's my client."

"I'm aware." He tilts his head to the side. "I asked how he became your *friend*."

"He became my *client* after I met him at a social event."

He clasps his hands together on the table. "I've known Giles for a very long time." His gaze meets mine, and I swear every time he looks me in the eye my breath seems to falter. "He has an awful weakness for pretty women, always has had, and yet he respects you. *He* see's *you* as a friend." Great, and now I feel guilty for denying that I like him, because I do, but this is business. Rule number four: You must always be above reproach. Don't give anyone the opportunity to question your professionalism. Giles is my sole exception, the only one for whom I even slightly blur the lines, but I don't want Landon Banks to know that. Something tells me that with him the lines are going to need to be two-foot wide, preferably with a razor wire topped fence running along them.

"I have a professional relationship with Giles. I embrace his friendly manner because that's just how he is. You have to be a chameleon to succeed in this world, Mr. Banks. I change according to my surroundings."

The longer I look at him, the more charged the air between us seems to become, like a battery powering up, a low hum fuelling it. My breath hitches as the power starts to fizz and crackle, sparking violently between us with such force that I have to focus very hard just so that I don't start subconsciously leaning across the table towards him.

"Careful Georgia. You need friends in this city. It can get lonely."

"It's lonely at the top." I manage to speak.

Still, his eyes burn into me and something flashes in their depths. "It can be."

The trance is broken when the waitress arrives at the table, placing two plates in front of us. I drop my gaze and feel the blush heating my cheeks. Dangerous. Landon Banks is dangerous. He's not like the other egotistical twats I usually have to deal with. I mean, he's egotistical, but he's intelligent, he see's too much. My standard intimidation mixed with some fake, sugar sweet bullshit won't work on him, and that's not good. At all. It leaves me wide open to him, and I can't afford that kind of exposure, not with a predator like him circling me.

10

LUNCH WITH LANDON yesterday was so awkward after our strange little interaction. He's infuriating, arrogant, obnoxious...and yet there's something about him, something that I'm drawn to. It's as though one wrong move might set off a reaction of epic proportions. I've decided I'm going to avoid him at all cost. He's only here for a few weeks, so it shouldn't be too hard.

The truth is, whether I like it or not, Landon has an effect on me. The over-whelming tension between us is dangerous in and of itself, a match that given any sort of attention may well just light itself before I've ever even realised it's happened. The thing that scares me the most about him though is that he makes me feel as though I have no control of the situation, and there's nothing I hate more than loss of control.

I take the lift up to the top floor and push open the heavy door open, stepping into the enormous glass office. Focusing my gaze on Angus, I walk in a straight line to his desk. I know Landon is sitting at his desk and I'm acutely aware of his eyes on me, but I refuse to look at him.

"Landon." I say, still refusing to look. "Angus."

I drop the latest figures on Angus' desk, and his gaze subtly shifts between me and Landon before he picks up the papers, glancing over them.

"Let me know if you need anything." I turn on my heel and walk back the way I came.

"What, that's it? No run down?" Angus asks, a hint of distress leaking into his voice. I pause and glance over my shoulder, catching a brief glimpse of Landon. His head is tilted forward studying something on the desk in front of him, but I don't miss the small quirk of his lips.

I narrow my eyes and plaster a smile on my face. "You don't need my run down, Angus. You're a better broker than I could ever hope to be." I charm for all I'm fucking worth.

I walk out, closing the door behind me, and just before the latch clicks in place I hear a loud bang from inside, followed by Angus hissing. "Did you fuck her?!"

"What? No! Of course not." Landon says before I walk away. Okay, so I need to work on my avoidance strategy. I can do this, I've spent five years acting my arse off, playing the game like it's a fine art. This is no different, it's all just part of the game, and I will become the damn master if it kills me. The next time I see Angus or Landon for that matter, all they will see is cool, calm, professional, because that's what I am.

My two o' clock meeting is with one of the clients that came with me from Elite. I really wish he hadn't to be honest. I hate dealing with him.

Charles Thomas is one of those guys that makes your skin crawl with just a look. He defines sleazy and gross. He must be well in his seventies and spends half his life in Spain, as a result he looks like a shrivelled apricot.

I step into the conference room and take a seat opposite him. He smiles wide, revealing perfectly white veneers made even whiter against his tanned leathery skin. He's wearing a bloody Hawaiian shirt, as though making it clear to the world that he's retired and living somewhere hot unlike us poor fucks. Although if I had his money, I'm pretty sure the Caribbean would be on the cards, not Spain.

"Miss Roberts," he says, sounding every bit as creepy as he looks.

"Mr. Thomas." I hide my disdain behind a bright and shiny smile.

I open his investment portfolio and turn it around, pushing it in front of him. "You wanted to discuss some new investments..." I start when the door pushes open. I glare at the culprit who is interrupting my meeting, and my glare only intensifies when I see Landon step into the room, instantly consuming every inch of it with that confidence of his.

"Mr. Thomas," he says, and the old man rises to his feet with a groan, before shaking Landon's hand. "Landon Banks." He introduces himself.

"Ah, the man at the helm." Thomas chuckles to himself.

"Sorry I'm late."

"Oh, you're not," I grate. You're not late because you're not supposed to be here, now fuck off! God, I wish I could say that.

Landon rounds the conference table with that predatory grace he wears so well, taking a seat next to me. He turns slightly, angling his body towards me. My skin prickles with awareness, and I take a steadying breath.

"As I was saying Mr. Thomas, here are my proposed

suggestions for you. Each company has its merits depending on what you want. One through three are three to five year turnover investments, turning a more secure profit around the five percent range." He nods, holding his chin between his thumb and index finger as he reads the document I carefully prepared. Landon reaches out and takes the file from in front of me. I scowl at him and he smirks, keeping his eyes fixed on me as he opens it. I clear my throat and focus. "Options three through seven are longer term investments, ten year investments that may return up to fifteen percent." He looks up at me, smiling.

"Well, I like fifteen percent."

I hold up a hand, halting him. "Yes, but as you know with a ten-year investment, the market could fluctuate massively."

"In order to win, you have to take risks." Landon throws in, closing the folder and chucking it haphazardly onto the desk. He props his elbow on the table, twisting his body to face me even more. We stare at each other for a few seconds, until he cocks his eyebrow.

"The decision is yours, Mr. Thomas. By all means, take the proposal and read it over." I try to urge caution because I know exactly where this is going. Landon comes in here with his expensive suit, his good looks and his 'I own the world' attitude, and basically throws down with 'In order to win you have to take risks'. In man speak this is, look how big my dick is. I'm a risk taker. I'm a winner. What are you going to be? And you'd think Thomas is old enough to know better...

"No, Mr. Banks is right. No point in playing it safe. I'll transfer funds to you this afternoon. Pick whichever you think is best and go all in." He says, shaking his head as he closes his file, and stands.

Oh my god. I stand and shake his hand, trying to hide my disapproval as I watch him walk out of the office with a slight limp. The second the door clicks shut I round on Landon who is still lounging in the chair, his thighs spread casually and his head lolling over the back as though this entire thing bores him.

I lean over, grabbing the arms of his chair, and bringing my face close to his. "What the hell are you doing in *my* meeting?"

He lifts his head, bringing his lips a whisper from mine. "This is my firm, Miss Roberts, and I'm well within my rights to oversee my staff." My grip on the chair tightens, my nails pressing against the plastic until a dull throb starts in my cuticles. I think my eye is twitching. Yep, it's definitely twitching.

"So, I need overseeing now?" My voice is low and careful, my words designed to provoke him to think before he fucks me off.

I refuse to back down, even when I can feel his warm breath blowing over my lips. "You weren't going to close that." His eyes lock with mine, and it's as though there's a physical force pushing against me, demanding I back off, back down. Screw that.

"I don't need to pull my cock out to get a client to invest."

His eyes dance with amusement and the corner of his lips twitches. "Well, that would be a feat, Georgia. A disappointing one at that."

"You might be my boss, but these are my clients, clients *I* brought to your firm." The smirk slips from his lips.

"Seems as though the kitten has her claws out today." His gaze locks with mine in a tense stand off. The air shifts and my pulse picks up. I hadn't realised how close to him I was until now, until my tongue darts over my dry lips, drawing his eyes to my mouth where it remains.

I'm caught in a snare, being hopelessly drawn to him and imagining what it would feel like to have those full lips against mine, his strong hands around my waist, in my hair.

His gaze drops further to my chest, and I realise he must have a clear view straight down my blouse. And suddenly it's too close, too much. I'm a hairs breath away from doing something stupid. I blink and straighten, staggering back a step. I squeeze my eyes shut, before turning and picking up the folders off the table, clutching them against my chest as if they can somehow shield me from him.

"I'm not a kitten, Mr. Banks. You'd do well to remember it." I storm out of the conference room, slamming the door behind me. Only once I'm outside do I take the heaving breath that I'm so desperately in need of. So much for avoiding him. Shit.

11

THE REST of the week is torturous. Landon turns up in another one of my meetings. He pushes my buttons and thus pulls my strings like I'm his very own puppet. Yet each morning I go to see Angus and Landon sits there without saying a word whilst I attempt to completely ignore him. On the outside it works. I don't even glance his way, but in reality it's a completely different story. I'm hyper aware of him, my body jumping to attention at his mere presence. I hate it, but I have no control over it. It's a visceral reaction. A bone deep pull so primal that it's etched into my very DNA. There's nothing rational or even conscious about it, it just is. I'm attracted to Landon Banks in ways I didn't even think were possible. Trust me, I hate everything about this, and I'm sure to make it clear whenever I have to interact with the bastard. Angus glances between the two of us, and I can see him trying to work out what the hell is going on.

I've just left one such awkward interaction and am in my office when there's a knock at the door. "Come in!" I shout.

The door cracks open and Angus pops his head through the gap. "Do you have a minute?"

"Of course." I gesture to the chair on the opposite side of my desk and he closes the door before taking the seat, perching on the edge.

He opens his mouth to start speaking and then closes it again. I cock a brow, waiting for him to say what he has to say, but he looks...embarrassed.

"Okay. I don't mean this offensively, but is there something going on with you and Landon?" he blurts.

My eyes widen. "No!"

He holds his hands up. "Not that I'm prying," he says in a rush. "It's fine if you are, but you're both acting very strange, and I don't want you to leave us. You know, after your last boss." I never told Angus about Collins, so either that came from Giles or he believes the bullshit rumours and thinks I screwed Collins. Brilliant.

I grab a handful of papers on the desk and start shuffling them, simply so I can avoid having to look at him through this mortifying conversation, only made worse by the fact that Angus looks like he wants to crawl into the deepest darkest hole he can find and never come out.

I finally lift my gaze to his. "I can honestly say that I would never sleep with anyone inside of this building, Angus. You have my word on that."

He nods, dropping his gaze to his lap. "Okay, good. That's... that's good."

"Great, so we're okay?"

He nods stiffly, a frown pinching his brows together as he scrubs a hand over his short beard. "If that's not it though, then why *are* you so off with him?"

"Honestly?" He nods, waiting for me to make some great revelation. "I just don't like him."

He bursts out laughing, throwing his head back and pressing one hand to his stomach. "Amazing. I knew I liked you for a reason, Georgia. I'll see you at one for that lunch meeting." He pushes up from the chair, buttoning his suit jacket.

"I'll be there."

He ducks his head as if he's giving me a little bow before he turns and walks out of the room. I smile. Angus is an odd man, but also one of the most genuine, a trait that's hard to come by in this business.

***

I step inside the restaurant at twelve forty-five, scanning the room for Angus and Giles. Giles just sold his park side apartment in New York and he's pushing for huge investment with the money. We want the best shot for him, so Angus and I have both come up with separate proposals.

Of course, if we have to lunch clients then we have to do it properly. This place is just around the corner from the office and serves French food. Contemporary music drifts around the room. My heels sound entirely too loud on the stone floor as I walk in.

"Oh, this is nice. I've never been here." Eva comments beside me. I've brought her along because, well, she asked if she could come and I've become quite fond of her. It's Giles, so I know he won't care, and she can take notes or something.

I hear Giles before I see him, his booming laugh sounding around the large room. I follow the sound to the bar, where he's cradling a glass of wine and talking to Landon. *Landon.* What the fuck is he doing here?

I approach them, being sure to glare at Landon when he looks my way. "Giles. How are you?" I ask, allowing him to embrace me and kiss my cheek.

"Ah, Georgia, darling. I'm very well. You look beautiful."
The man could charm the birds out of the sky.

"Thank you. Giles, this is my assistant, Eva."

He takes her hand, kissing the back of it, his lips
lingering as a small smile forms on his lips. I roll my eyes
and shake my head. "Another beautiful one," he says before
turning to Landon. "We're lucky to have such company."

Landon fixes his gaze on mine. "Indeed we are."

That *thing* flutters in my stomach and the invisible
weight that only materialises around him presses on my
chest. "I didn't realise we had the pleasure of your company
today," I say, leaking just enough acid into my voice to let
him know I hate him.

He flashes me that wry smile. "I just like to catch you off
guard, Ms. Roberts."

I feign a small laugh, before pointedly resuming my
scowl for a moment and turning away from him.

A waitress approaches us. "Your table is ready. If you'd
like to follow me."

Giles follows after her and I'm pretty sure he's staring
at her arse. She leads us to a table right next to the
window. Landon brushes against me, pulling a chair out
and gesturing for me to sit. I begrudgingly do and he
pushes the chair in behind me. I'm hyper aware of him
standing right behind me and a small shiver moves over
my body, as if anticipating that he might touch me. Of
course he moves away, sitting beside me. He takes the
bottle of wine from the ice bucket in the middle of the
table and pours me a glass before pouring another and
passing it to Giles.

"Thank you." I say quietly. Eva and Giles are chatting to
themselves and she has her back slightly turned to me.

Landon and I sit silently until he breaks the reigning

awkwardness. "Angus should be here in a moment. He got tied up."

"Good."

He leans into my side, so close that his arm brushes against mine. "Did I do something to upset you, kitten?"

I turn to face him, my gaze meeting his. "Call me kitten again and we're going to have a problem."

Those perfectly full lips pull into a smirk. "Tell me, is it just me you dislike so much, or are you this delightful with everyone?"

I pick up my glass and twirl the stem between my fingers. "I have no idea what you're talking about, Mr. Banks. I simply like to keep clear professional boundaries."

"Of course, boundaries are so easily crossed when dealing with someone as uptight as yourself."

I whip my head around to face him. "I am not uptight."

He leans in, bringing his face closer to mine, until I can actually feel his breath on my skin. "I beg to differ," he whispers as his eyes flick down to my lips. That *thing* starts to simmer between us, filling the space with a certain expectation. My heart hammers against my ribs, and my breathing picks up until my chest feels too small for my lungs.

Someone clears a throat loudly and I jump back and focus on the table, willing the heat to disappear from my cheeks.

"Landon..." Giles starts, engaging him in easy conversation. It's muted by the roar in my ears. This is ridiculous. He goads me, and every time I fall into it.

"Is that some kind of foreplay?" Eva whispers, leaning sideways and bringing her lips close to my ear.

"No!"

She snorts and holds her hands up, still smiling.

Then Angus turns up and starts looking between me

and Landon like we're about to mount each other. Oh my fucking god. I cannot deal with this.

"Lets get down to business shall we?" I say, already exasperated and we haven't even begun.

"Of course," Landon replies, his voice dropping into something sensual and gritty.

I clench my jaw and dig my nails into my palm hard enough to cause a bite of pain. I feel as if everyone is looking at us, waiting for something. Brilliant. Shoot me now.

12

ONE WEEK. It's been one week since I was first introduced to Landon and I'm a woman on the edge. I must have fantasised at least a hundred times about bending him over and ploughing him with The Destroyer, just to make him my bitch.

As soon as I get home on Friday evening, I strip out of my pencil skirt and blouse, before I get in the shower. I let the hot water pummel my back, easing the knots formed by days of tension. When I'm done, I throw on a white dress with cut out's in the sides. I would never normally wear something so risqué, but tonight I need to blow off steam. I curl my blonde hair until it falls loosely around my shoulders and put my make-up on, finishing it with some bright red lipstick.

I meet Quinn and Eva in front of Q, because yes, she asked if she could come. I wouldn't usually socialise with someone I work so closely with, but I really like her

We bypass the queue waiting to get in Q and duck down a side alley that leads to the back of the building. A lone black door is guarded by a bouncer, and to anyone who knows otherwise, it simply looks like a back entrance to Q.

The bouncer eyes Quinn and Eva as we approach the door.

"They're with me." I say, typing the code into the keypad beside the door. It beeps and the small red light turns green.

We step inside and descend the short flight of stairs, dimly lit with LED's on each step.

"Holy shit, is this some freaky sex club or something?" Eva asks, causing Quinn and I to exchange glances.

"No, that's later." Quinn says, making Eva laugh. Little does she know.

As soon as we step inside The Mayfair Bar we move over to one of the seating booths. The club is always dark, the bar lit only by the up-lighting that showcases the wall of top shelf liquors behind it. The seating is comprised of little round booths set back into the walls, each one with a sheer black curtain that pulls across, giving the illusion of privacy. Even the chandeliers that hang over each booth are covered in black netting, dimming the light.

This is a private club as such, not quite as private as Masque, but it requires a membership to get in. It sits in the basement below Q, one of the most exclusive nightclubs in the city. Basically, around here, you have to be someone or know someone or you aren't getting in anywhere. The people that come here are the high rollers, the top of the food chain as it were. And one such person happened to be a client of mine. He gotme the membership here as a thank you for turning an extra three percent on his forecast.

The waiter brings our drinks only minutes after we order, and I hand him three fifties, making eye contact as I do. He nods and shoves his hand in the pocket of his blazer, producing three small bags of white powder. Mexy. The very reason that Quinn and I are able to out-play the boys so well. It counteracts the effects of alcohol, stops you from becoming drunk and sloppy, as well as sharpening the senses.

Rule number four: You must be above reproach. Getting drunk is not how we do things, but not drinking is simply not an option, not if I'm going to keep my sanity. I give you Mexy; a legal high. The emphasis being on legal. It costs about the same as Cocaine, but gone are the days when merchant bankers could live on blow, make shit tons of money and expect the boss to turn a blind eye. I pick up my glass of vodka, the outside misted from the ice cold liquid, and neck the shot.

"I'll be right back." I push up from the table and go to the bathroom, clutching the little bag of white powder in my palm. As much as I'm in the mood to get completely smashed, it's never a good move. Party as hard as you like, but never get messy, because no matter how hard they play, no one likes a messy, slurring bitch. I pull the small mirror from my clutch and set out a line of the white powder before snorting it. It instantly sharpens my senses. I check my reflection and leave the bathroom. I'm halfway back to my table when I hear a rumble of laughter from a nearby table. I spot a table of four men, all in expensive suits, glasses of whiskey in front of them and a bottle in the middle of the table. Their faces are shrouded in shadow and two of them are smoking cigars, the clouds of smoke lingering in the air heavily. Gangsters come to mind. A couple of them glance at me as I move past, a few feet from their booth. It's very much like predators sizing each other up, trying to work out just how much of a power player the other is.

"Georgia?"

I pause, closing my eyes and praying that my ears are deceiving me and it's not *his* voice.

I squint through the shadows at Landon as three other sets of curious eyes watch us. I try to escape him, come out to unwind and of course I bump into him, in the very bar that I frequent to ensure I don't run into any unwanted *friends*.

"Landon." He's sat across the circular booth, forearms braced on the table. His usual jacket is missing and the sleeves of his shirt are rolled up, revealing tanned, muscular forearms. I force myself not to ogle his arms, and his gaze slams into mine and for a second my chest actually feels paralyzed, like the breath is physically stuck in my lungs. He tilts his head in that way of his, like he's sizing up his prey.

"Why don't you join us, sweetheart?" One of the guys asks. I glance at him briefly. Wealthy, entitled and sleazy— and friends with my boss. I really did not want this shit tonight.

"That's kind of you, but I'm here with someone." I paint a fake smile on my face.

"Well bring them on over." He insists, flicking his eyes to my cleavage.

I sigh and pray for a little patience. *Do not tell him to fuck off,* I repeat in my mind like a mantra. I'm starting to think that I have some very real issues with tolerance.

I'm about to come up with another bullshit excuse when Landon chips in. "She doesn't want to suck your dick, Denton."

"She might." He sneers, clearly feeling as though his balls are enormous while he's sat with his friends.

"I assure you, I really don't." I see the tell tale signs of a bruised male ego as the smile slowly slips from his lips. "I'm not into cock."

His eyebrows shoot up and the smile returns. "Is that so?" Well, technically I'm not into sucking dick, now putting a dick in him...that I would do.

I can feel Landon's eyes on me as I turn away. "Have a good night boys," I throw over my shoulder as a parting comment. Quinn has finished her drink and is tapping her foot impatiently when I get back. Eva is on her phone.

"Sorry. Bumped into someone."

"Okay. We'll be back." She says, scooping up her clutch bag and leaving the table with Eva in tow. I drum my fingers over the table as agitation crawls over me. I don't know what it is. I always keep my cool. Always. And suddenly I hate everything. I want to go dancing, have a night of wild sex, something, anything. A figure moves from the shadows beside the table and drops into the seat that Quinn just vacated. Landon.

"You're high," he says.

I'm nit going to deny it. "It's legal and therefore none of your business."

I can tell he's fighting a smile. "Just a passing comment."

"Okay, I'm going to propose something," I tell him.

He leans forward, resting his elbows on the table. "I'm listening."

"You are my boss. I am your employee. That's it. Let's not pretend we want to socialise or have a conversation, and let's not make passing comments." The buzz racing through my veins is making me brave, but weirdly I don't feel like I'm walking a fine line saying this to him. I might not like him, but he's not the kind of guy who would reprimand honesty.

"Well, I would agree to it if it were true." He says.

I frown. "What?"

"You say we don't want to socialise or have a conversation and it's not true. I'm very interested in having a conversation with you, Georgia. You really only have yourself to blame. One minute you're the appeasing model employee and the next the real you comes out to play with her claws out."

"You bring out the worst in me."

He huffs a laugh. "No, I just dig a little deeper than the bullshit front you put on."

His eyes burn into mine and I can feel my temper rising like an angry snake. "There is no front, and this isn't a game. This is my job, my life. Do you have any idea how hard I have worked to get where I am?"

He presses his lips together. "I can imagine."

I laugh, because, really? "No, you can't. Every step I have taken to get here is carefully orchestrated. You wanted to know why I left Elite. Collins hit on me. Got drunk and cornered me in the bathroom at the office party." I have no idea why I'm telling him this. "I don't want to be the woman who takes home a good wage, I want to be the best. I can't be the best under a boss who sees me as something to sink his dick in now, can I?" I'm not even talking about him, or maybe I am, but something shifts in his eyes that makes me think that suddenly we are.

"Angus doesn't want to sink his dick in you." The implication of his words hang unfinished in the air. *But I do.* Or maybe it's just wishful thinking from my ovaries again.

"Angus isn't my only boss." Bold, too bold. The words hang in the air.

He leans forward, propping his elbows on the table, and I find myself doing the same, as if we're negotiating a business meeting. "You ask a lot, kitten." I don't know what that even means. I ask for nothing. I *want* nothing.

"I ask for respect."

He cocks a brow. "You have it, and believe me when I say that not many can say the same."

I open my mouth to respond when Quinn appears with Eva right beside her. His gaze holds mine as he pushes to his feet.

"Have a good evening, ladies." He says, smiling briefly at Quinn and Eva before he departs.

As always, I have to release the breath I've been holding when he leaves.

Quinn watches him go, before sitting down and turning her wide eyes on me. "*That* is Landon Banks?" I nod. "Holy fuck." She starts fanning herself.

"I know, right?" Eva joins in. "I wish I was *his* assistant." She shoots a look at me "Oh, no offense, G, but you know, you're kind of lacking some of his appeal."

I ignore them both, watching as Landon moves through the shadows of the bar. I fight with myself for long moments, and then I'm pushing to my feet and striding across the room. He's almost at his table when I call his name.

He turns to face me and I jerk my head in the direction of the back of the bar. He follows me to a hallway that leads to a fire exit, tucked away beside the lift. I stop and pivot on my heel, crossing my arms over my chest as I face him. He watches me carefully, his expression blank.

"I don't like you." I tell him.

He laughs as he folds his arms over his chest, mimicking my stance. "Say how you really feel why don't you."

"And you don't like me." I continue.

He holds up a finger. "I like *you*. I don't like the shit you put on for everyone else."

I huff, but really I want to scream. "I don't put on anything. I'm just nice to other people. This needs to stop, this...issue ...that we have." I gesture between us. "Angus is noticing."

He closes the short distance between us, a wicked smile curving his lips. I drop my gaze to his chest in an attempt to avoid looking at him. "I'm not the one who's worried about my precious image."

I pinch the bridge of my nose, praying for patience. "Landon, please."

His finger brushes beneath my chin and I freeze as he tilts my face up, bringing my gaze to his. I hold my breath as long seconds pass. When he drops his hand, I miss the heat of his touch. "Fine, I'll stop on one condition."

"What?"

"Cut the bullshit. It irritates me, you know it does." I want to slap him, but instead I bite my tongue.

"Okay, I will ensure that to you, I unleash my inner bitch at all times."

"Good, then we have a truce." He holds out his hand to me and I take it. Fingers crossed this works.

13

THE NEXT WEEK IS QUIET, non-eventful. I barely see Landon and my life returns to the way it was before he disrupted it. I fall back into my usual routine: morning workout, work, play, sleep and repeat.

My email pings, and it's from Giles. I scan over the document detailing some new Middle East investment, which probably involves oil. There's no such thing as a sure thing when it comes to investments but oil is as close as it gets. Every broker has a list of companies it deals with though, and that's Landon's thing, so he'll have to approve it. I hit Google, and research the details, putting together a folder.

When I step out of the lift for the boys' office, the secretary is gone. She's never gone. Hell I was starting to doubt whether the woman ever went home. I frown as I move past her empty desk and knock on the door to the office. Nothing. Silence. I push the door open and slip inside, walking to Landon's desk, the folder clutched against my chest. I drop it on the carnage that is his desk, and I want to walk away, but my OCD can't cope. I mean, shit, I leave stuff on my desk, in a neat pile, organised. This just looks like something exploded in here.

I sigh and start picking up the loose papers that are scattered everywhere. I gather the separate pieces of a document, scanning the print and putting them in order.

Something touches my shoulder. I jump and squeal, whirling around and staggering into Landon. My nose brushes against the material of his jacket and papers fly everywhere. The only thing saving me from face planting his chest are the hands he wraps firmly around my waist.

"Shit. You scared me!"

A low chuckle escapes his throat, and I shiver, tilting my head back so I can look up at him.

He cocks a brow. "Sorry."

I'm caught off guard and my breath hitches violently, my heart rate speeding, anticipating...something. Anything. I can feel his breath on my face, smell the intoxicating scent of his aftershave, feel the heat of his body pressed against mine, his palms burning through my dress in a way that makes me feel branded. It all comes flooding in like a tidal wave, my senses becoming overwhelmed with him, craving him like a junkie craves a long lost fix.

His eyes flash with something dark and dangerous before they drop to my lips, and unlike every other time he's looked at me since we called our strange truce, he doesn't immediately tear them away, instead focusing on them completely. My pulse starts to hammer so hard it's like a drum beat in my ears, the rhythmic pounding getting faster and faster. The space between us becomes charged.

His gaze flicks briefly to mine and that's when I see it, the indecision. His fingers twitch, reminding me that his hands are still on my waist, reminding me that they shouldn't be. I try and find the willpower to move away from his hard body at the exact same time that I see the resolve harden in his eyes. I barely have time to register it, to do anything before one hand fists my hair and his lips slam over mine. I can't breathe, can't move, can't think. His kiss is violent, demanding and teasing at the same time.

I try to remember why this is wrong, but his mouth feels so good on mine. His grip on my hair tightens and I gasp, allowing him to slide his tongue inside my mouth. My fingers are clinging to handfuls of his shirt, pulling him closer? Pushing him away? I don't even know. Its tongue and teeth, a dirty promise, a sweet threat of what could come.

He releases my hair and both hands span my waist, lifting me and tossing me roughly on the desk before he steps between my legs, forcing the material of my dress to creep up my thighs. And I let him, because this craving, this want; it's a creature that his been clawing at my chest for weeks. And its chains have finally broken. A small voice in the back of my mind tells me to cage it again, to stop, but he's like a drug, burning through my veins. The soft caress of his suit trousers brushes against the inside of my thighs, followed my the brush of his fingers against the lace of my underwear. Angus could walk in here, the secretary. The thought makes me falter for a second, but it's long enough to break the madness. I tear my lips from his, and press my hand against his chest, keeping my fingers closed in a tight fist, as though touching him too much is dangerous, and honestly, it is. I close my eyes and refuse to look at him, because I just kissed my fucking boss. His fingers wrap around my wrist, holding my hand to his chest. I can feel his hot breath blowing across my scalp as I try to catch my breath.

"Shit." I breathe. *Shit, shit, shit.* This changes everything. Every-fucking-thing. I yank my hand away from his grasp and drag it through my hair. "Fucking shit." I push off the desk and try to move around him, but he grabs my chin, forcing me to look at him. His gaze locks with mine, a frown marring his features as his nostrils flare. I wait for him to say something, but instead he simply releases me, trailing his fingers over my neck as he drops his hand back to his side.

I force myself to turn away and walk out, because whatever just happened is bad, really bad, but it could be worse. I need to walk away while all my clothes are still on.

I meet Quinn at the little hole in the wall bar a few streets over from her offices. It's quiet at this time, with only the odd customer dotted around the tables.

Quinn sits in her office attire looking every bit the badass solicitor she is. A Cosmopolitan is in front of her and a Martini waits for me.

"So, emergency meeting? Colour me intrigued." She says as I take the seat across from her.

I shake my head and take the olive out of my martini, popping it inside my mouth and twirling the cocktail stick between my fingers as I chew. "I did something stupid."

"Landon Banks stupid?"

I groan and drop my head into my hands. "Maybe."

She grabs my wrist, yanking my hand away from my face. "Are you serious?" A frown mars her features.

God, I wish I could say no, that there is no way I would be that stupid, but I came here for advice. "We kissed." I drop my gaze to the glass in front of me, pick it up, and down half of it in one gulp.

When I look up, her lips are pressed together in a firm

line. "You kissed?" I nod. "Landon Banks?" I nod again. "What happened to the pact?"

"I don't fucking know. We were fine, it was fine. And then I go to his office and he crept up on me. It was a surprise stealth attack."

She leans forward, bracing her palms flat against the table top and looking me in the eye. "Okay, but you didn't fuck him?"

"No. It got...heated." Her eyes pop wide. "But I stopped it!" I defend. God, when did I become *that* girl?

She picks up her drink and takes a sip. "He looks at you like he's seen your pussy."

"Helpful."

She shrugs. "So, when are you handing in your notice?"

How was I so stupid? If I leave Banks and Redford now, it'll look shit on my so far glowing CV. Fuck.

"No." I shake my head. "I think I can fix it, maybe." I mean, he made a pact with me didn't he? Granted he broke it, but he must have a certain degree of willingness not to fuck me over in every way.

She sighs. "Well shit, George. You don't make things easy on yourself."

"I know."

She drags a hand through her long dark hair and leans back in her seat. "Look, I know you. It must have taken a lot for you to break rank, so..."

"So what?" I snap, this entire situation making me agitated. I pick up my martini and take another heavy gulp.

"I think you should fuck him."

I inhale sharply and choke on a lungful of vodka. "What the hell, Quinn?!" I cough violently and smack my hand against my chest.

She holds her hand up. "I've seen you together for all of

five seconds in your so called 'professional' mode, and I needed a cigarette just watching. If you can't control yourself enough to not kiss him, then it's only a matter of time before he has you bent over his desk."

I shake my head. "No, never. There's a big fat line between kissing him and fucking him."

A group of businessman move past our table and Quinn leans forward, keeping her voice low. "There's a big fat line between your boss and his tongue."

"Okay then, genius, tell me how you would get out of this—preferably without sleeping with him."

She lifts her drink to her lips. "Fuck him or quit."

"Wow." I shake my head. "You want me to end up jobless. You're a terrible friend."

"Look, I guarantee, one way or the other, you are going to do it. You can let him control the where, when and how, or you can." She's insane. We have one major rule. Do not fuck your boss. Not, do not fuck your boss unless he's sexy as all hell and you really want to.

"You want me to invite him back to my apartment and just go to town on him?"

"Or...you could invite him to Masque?"

I freeze as the thought that shouldn't even be a thought begins to take hold. I hate the idea of fucking him, of being that person, but when I imagine it, the act, not the reasoning, just the physical act of fucking Landon, I have to clench my thighs together. My heart rate speeds as I think of Landon between my legs, driving into me. I swipe my sweaty palms over the skirt of my dress, the skirt that a few hours ago was shoved up around my thighs. Shit. The idea both scares and excites me. I play by a set of rules for a reason, to succeed. I have lived and breathed those rules for years, always striving to be the best, and now...now I'm faced with the forbidden fruit, my boss, my hot boss. My rules were broken the second his lips touched mine, and even in my denial, I know I'm screwed either way.

They say that rules were made to be broken, but what about bent? No one said anything about that.

14

I GO to the office early with one task in mind. There are only a couple of people on my floor, and I move between the cubicles that are spread wall to wall, making my way to my office. Eva isn't in yet, because of course, I'm not even usually in at this time.

I drop my handbag on my desk and pace in front of it, watching the sun creep between the London sky scrapers, reflecting off the glass and painting the sky in hues of orange and peach.

I have gone backwards and forwards in my mind, changing my mind constantly.

The thing is, no matter how accomplished we are, no matter how intelligent, or seemingly rational, beneath it all, we're just animals. Our decisions are governed by instinct, by primal reactions. Animal attraction. It can make you do things you never thought you would, because that kind of all consuming chemistry is life's natural high, a spike of adrenaline in the mediocrity of life.

I have fucked countless men and met many more, but only one has had the ability to make me want him with this debilitating need. That is why I'm here, because when someone as powerful as Landon Banks walks into your life, it's not rational. It's barely human.

So what do I do? I try my best to cage the beast, to control it and manipulate it. Am I likely to get bitten in the process? Of course.

I open my bag and take out my purse, sliding a simple black card out, and glancing over the gold leaf writing. I take a steadying breath. If I do this, there is no going back, my intentions have been made clear.

Fuck it. I've always taken anything I've wanted, and as much as I try to pretend otherwise, I want Landon Banks.

I print off the daily report and take the elevator up to Landon and Angus' office. The secretary, Susan is here as always, excluding the one time when my boss decided to facially assault me of course.

"They're not in yet, dear," she says, looking up from her desk.

"I'll just leave this for them." I hold up the morning print out up to show her before opening the office door.

The sun pours through the glass walls, making the room look like some kind of palace.

I pop the card on Landon's desk and then pause, staring at the innocent little black and gold rectangle for a second. Masque is emblazoned across the front with a small logo of a masquerade mask and a web address, while on the back, embedded into the thick card is the gold lettering with the password: Tigress.

At the moment I have plausible deniability. I didn't want him to kiss me. It was a mistake, the list is endless, but the second I leave this card for him, there is no more denying this crazy sexual attraction between us.

I know this is a farce. Why don't I just fuck him like a

normal person? Ask him out? Because there's breaking the rules and there's manipulating them. Blatantly fucking your boss in the office, well, I might as well just hand in my resignation right now. All sorts of people go to Masque. For all I know, Apollo could be a CEO, a client, anyone. That's the beauty of anonymity. Yes, I'm inviting Landon to a club so I can fuck him, but once there, he could be anyone. I have plausible deniability, even if it is just the excuse I need. After all, while we're in those walls, we aren't Landon and Georgia, employer and employee, we are simply two consenting adults. The tigress and her prey. I'll fuck whatever this is out of my system and then it's done, and I can go on with my life pretending it never happened.

Before I can lose my nerve, I turn and walk out of his office, flashing a smile at Susan as I pass. I press the button for the lift, and wait, inspecting a chip in my nail polish. The doors ping open and I start to step forward before I lift my gaze and come face to face with Landon. We really need to stop meeting like this. He steps out of the lift, bringing himself far too close to me to be professional.

"Georgia." His voice low and deep, caressing my name like it's foreplay.

"Landon." I reply with false confidence. I edge around him, putting a little more space between us. My heart stutters in my chest, my body reacting to him involuntarily, as though the taste of his lips has opened the flood gates. I want to slap myself for being so pathetic. "I left the latest figures on your desk," I say quickly before stepping into the lift.

I allow my eyes to sweep over his body just before the doors glide shut. Damn, he makes that suit look so good. He makes everything look good. He turns me into a puddle, and yet, he's constantly surrounded by this calm, unwavering patience, like he knows I'll come to him eventually. And I guess I just did, masked and unwilling to acknowledge him.

As soon as I get into my office, I slam the door and press my back against it. He's probably typing the website address into his computer right now, reading the cryptic invitation that can only be accessed via the website and a password which is unique to each member. One spare pass. Each member gets one extra pass to use in a year, and I just gave mine to him.

I have tried to avoid this, I really have. I've ignored him. Remained professional. Even fucked Apollo whilst imagining it's him I'm ploughing through. My vibrator has had three battery changes in the last two weeks for Christ sake. He's here for another four weeks. I can't. I have never given up or admitted defeat in my entire life, but I am officially holding up the white flag.

I'll meet him at the club *just once*. I'll get him out of my system, maybe we'll just hate fuck the shit out of each other, and then I'll be able to survive the remaining four weeks. He'll leave and all will go back to normal.

The taxi pulls up outside Masque and I hand the driver some money before sliding out and slamming the door behind me.

I approach the entrance of the London town house and take out my mask, tying it into place and fluffing my hair over the delicate ribbons. My hand pauses, hovering over the huge brass knocker that adorns the glossy black wood door. My heart pounds against my ribs so hard it feels as though it's going to jump right out of my chest.

I knock and the guy in the suit answers, glancing at the

membership card in my outstretched hand and gesturing me inside.

The club has its usual vibe, rock music mixed with surroundings that would make even the wealthiest here green with envy. The bartender smiles at me as I approach the bar and begins making me a martini before I've even asked. He doesn't know me, of course he doesn't, but I'm the girl in the tiger mask and that's enough. He slides the drink in front of me and I remove the little cocktail stick, popping the olive in my mouth. My eyes flick around the room as I perch on the bar stool. It's almost midnight and the club is in full swing. I watch as a girl lies on her back on one of the leather chesterfield sofas, gripping the thighs of another girl who is riding her face. A couple of guys are watching, one appraising them as if they're a fascinating piece of art, and the other with his cock in his hand. Some might think that this is sleazy, but I think it's liberating.

My gaze shifts past the girls to the other side of the room where a figure has just walked in, his posture strong and confident. The upper half of his face covered by a black mask. The second he steps into any room, he fills it with an overwhelming energy. The way he moves, simply the way he stands oozes power, a power that cannot possibly be disguised. That mask is doing nothing to hide his identity.

His gaze meets mine and I hold it for a few seconds before turning away and picking up my drink, downing half of it to calm my nerves. He came, which means he wants me as much as I want him. I feel when he moves up beside me and slowly turn my gaze towards him.

"Whiskey," he tells the waiting bartender.

The silence hangs in the air between us before he turns towards me. "You surprise me."

I shrug one shoulder. "You underestimate me. It's not the same."

He takes the whiskey from the bartender and puts it to his lips, swallowing heavily. I watch his Adam's apple bob beneath the stubble covered skin of his throat and have to force myself to tear my eyes away. I almost jump when I feel his chest brush against my arm. "Georgia." His voice is laced with the threat of...something.

I turn towards him and our faces are so close that I can feel his whisky tinged breath on my lips. "No names."

"Is that why you wanted me to come here?" He trails his fingers up my arm and goosebumps explode over my skin. "So you could become a woman with no name?"

"I invited you here because I want to fuck you, and you want to fuck me. Here there are no names, no complications. Just sex. This is a one-time thing, no questions asked. And once we're done here, nothing changes." My gaze drops to his lips, and instinct screams at me to stop, but of course, the rules no longer apply. I broke them the second I placed that card on his desk, and now he's here. I might as well have already fucked him, because the damage is done. My boss knows I want to fuck him.

His lips kick up on one side and his fingers move from the top of my arm, up the side of my throat and into my hair. He gently grips a handful of it and pulls, tilting my head back. My pulse skitters wildly as my breath hitches in my throat.

He leans in, bringing his lips close to my ear. "Do you want me, kitten?" he rumbles, his voice maintaining that over whelming confidence that makes me weak in the knees.

I bite my lip, fighting the shiver that threatens to wrack my body when his breath touches my neck, but I refuse to answer him. And then his lips are on mine. I freeze for a second before my fingers are fisting handfuls of his jacket, pulling him closer. He spins me on the stool until my entire body is facing him, and then presses between my thighs. The material of his trousers brush against my sensitive skin and I tremble, imagining what it would feel like to have his hot skin against mine. His grip on my hair becomes almost painful. I gasp. He takes the opportunity to thrust his tongue inside my mouth. One hand moves from his jacket to the back of his neck, raking my nails over his skin.

He hisses over my lips and presses his forearm against the small of my back, dragging me off the stool. "Do you like to be watched?"

Our lips are barely millimetres apart, my ragged breath blowing across his lips. No man should be able to mess a girl up like this with just a kiss. "Not my thing."

I slip out from his hold and walk away without looking back at him, assuming he'll follow. My body is thrumming with excitement, desperate for his touch, but my mind is working at a million miles per hour. I don't want to be consumed by Landon Banks. I want to own him. I want to feel the control over him that I can't possibly have outside of this place. The question is, can a man like him even be controlled? Or would it be like keeping a lion as a pet and waiting for it to rip your arm off?

I walk up the stairs and chance a brief glance over my shoulder to find him right behind me. There are people everywhere in all sorts of positions. Men, women, three-somes, orgies, all going on right in the middle of the room, and yet his eyes remain focused on me.

I find a vacant room at the very end of the hall. He steps inside, his eyes flicking around the room quickly. I close the door and press my back against it, waiting. He turns to face me, a smirk on his lips as he tilts his head to the side slightly.

"Why did you invite me here?"

"Surely it's obvious?"

"Why *here* though?"

I shrug. "Plausible deniability. You're just a guy in a mask." Landon will never just be a guy in a mask though, as much as I wish he would be.

He laughs, the noise deep and rich. "You don't want to fuck me face to face."

When put like that I sound like such a coward. "No. I told you, I hate you."

His gaze slams into mine, that crippling intensity of his wrapping itself around me. He steps closer, pressing his body against mine and crushing me against the door, his forearm braced beside my head. He's so close, his lips are almost touching mine. A fissure of excitement rips through me at the want, the promise in his eyes. "You may wish to forget who I am, but some rules still apply," he whispers roughly. "Never lie to me."

I shove against his chest and force him back a couple of inches. "We're not in your office now, so I don't give a fuck about your bullshit rules." I decide to test the caged lion theory, and a small smile makes its way onto my lips. "You're nothing here."

His fingers snake up my neck, gripping my jaw in a bruising hold. "You think so?" His eyes flash with excitement.

I fight his hold, but it's pointless. "I know so. And by the way, I really do hate you."

A sick smile plays across his lips. "Oh, *Georgia*." I scowl at him, because I know he's only using my name to piss me off. "Do I need to tie you up and spank some of those anger problems out of you?"

I narrow my eyes, fixing them firmly on his, even as his fingers flinch, digging harder into my face. "I like to fuck jumped up little office boys with a strap-on until they beg me to stop." I cock a brow. I don't know what I was expecting, but it certainly isn't his wide grin.

"Of course you do."

The thought of bending Landon over and fucking him is alluring in ways that I cannot even explain. There's no man I'd love to have submit to me more than this one.

"Not going to happen, kitten, but I do love a fighter." His fingers work down my neck and he readjusts his grip around my throat, squeezing dangerously. "I will break you." Maybe that statement should scare me, but it doesn't.

I shove against him and he smirks. "Never."

"I have pictured fucking you so many times. Banding you. Breaking you." He leans in until his lips are at my ear. "You *will* submit to me, kitten." The low warning makes me tremble. I'm about to either call it off or kick him in the junk when his lips slam over mine so hard that my head slams back against the door. I try to twist my face away, but the hand around my throat pins me in place allowing me no movement. He thrusts his tongue inside my mouth and a bite him, making him rip his mouth away from me.

"Never." I repeat as the thrill of anticipation settles low in my stomach.

His eyes flash dangerously behind his mask before he releases his grip on my throat only to grab my dress and shred the material until it falls around my waist, exposing my bare breasts.

He leans forward, sucking one nipple into his hot

mouth. I moan and find myself pushing my chest into his face, wanting more, needing more.

His lips work upward, over my throat and jaw, until they brush my mouth. I'm too hot, my pulse hammering like a freight train through my veins as I try desperately to catch my breath. If this is a battle of wills, then I'm definitely losing. I grab the collar of his shirt, wrenching it open. The buttons scatter across the carpet like rain fall, and I get my first uninterrupted view of Landon Banks. Holy. Fuck.

His broad chest rises and falls on heavy breaths as he waits for me survey every inch of his exposed skin. His stomach looks like it was chiselled from stone, and I want to drag my tongue over it. I press my palm to the tanned skin of his chest, dragging it down, over each bump on his stomach until I brush the thin line of hair that drops below the waist of his trousers. He grabs my wrist. I barely have time to look up at his face before he twists my arm, forcing my chest up against the door painfully. His body hits my back and I can feel his warm breath on my neck as my shoulder screams in protest. It shouldn't be hot, it shouldn't send a shot of adrenaline racing through my veins and yet it does.

His fingertips gently trace the length of my thigh. When he brushes over the lace at the top of my stocking, he lets out a choked groan. He keeps going, dipping his hand between my legs. I keep them firmly closed and he presses his thigh between them, forcing them apart. His fingers slip beneath the scrap of material covering my pussy, dragging over me. I drop my head forward against the door, biting my lip to stop myself from moaning. So, he thrusts two fingers inside me without any warning, and I cry out.

"This feels an awful lot like submission."

"Submission is willing." I say, my breath hitching

desperately as he pulls out and pushes back in. I know I'm soaking wet.

He releases his hold on my arm, but his fingers remain buried in my pussy. "Feel free to leave at any time." He drags his tongue up the side of my neck and I bite back a moan. *Damn it, find some willpower, Georgia.* I place my palms against the door and squeeze my eyes shut, finding the resolve I'm apparently missing. I shove away from the door and turn around. His hand falls away from me in the process.

He lifts his fingers, showing them to me. "You don't want this?" He brings one finger to his lips and slides it inside his mouth, sucking it clean. "Say the word and this stops." His voice is low and guttural, triggering every hormone in my body to go haywire.

I want him. I've wanted him for weeks. But I want him on my terms. Landon doesn't work to terms though. This man cannot be dominated, but didn't I already know that long before I ever brought him up here? Landon Banks doesn't have a submissive bone in his body and we both know it. Maybe I secretly crave his brand of power and control.

Before I can overthink it, my lips collide with his. I rake my nails over the back of his neck, thrusting my tongue into his mouth. He groans against my lips, his hands skimming over my waist and gripping my arse, squeezing firmly. He lifts me until my thighs are wrapped around his body and his face is level with my breasts. He sucks one nipple into his mouth, lashing his tongue against it and skimming his teeth over me. I grip handfuls of his hair, pulling him closer and throwing my head back on a breathy moan.

The next thing I know, my back hits the mattress and he looms over me, watching with hungry eyes as he removes his shirt and then unfastens his belt. With every movement, every sound, my heart beat picks up, and when He stands there naked except for the mask covering half his face. His erection juts out in front of him, the thick veins wrapping around it in a map. He allows me to look my fill, and then his hands are on me, tearing my dress the rest of the way off. I'd complain if it wasn't turning me on so much. I've never had a man dominate everything like this and I'm not sure if I love or hate the lack of control.

His hands find my hips, and then he flips me over, throwing me face down against the satin sheets. I roll straight onto my back again, and rise onto my elbows, glaring up at him.

"Don't like it when you're the one getting fucked from behind?"

"I'll gladly fuck you. I have my strap-on in my bag. You'd probably love it." I smirk at him. "They always do."

He places a hand on the mattress either side of my body. His gaze flick between my eyes and my mouth. I find myself lifting my chin, bringing my face closer to his. His lips barely brush mine, his tongue swiping across my bottom lip before he grips my hips again.

"I'm good," he says against my lips before flipping me over again and fisting my hair in his hand. I gasp as he wrenches my head back hard, bowing my back so much that I have to brace on my outstretched hands. I feel the bed shift, and then his thighs are pressing against mine as he straddles me. He bites down on my earlobe, grinding his hard dick into my arse crack.

"Do you like *getting* fucked in the arse, *Georgia*?"

"I..." He grinds against me, dragging his dick all over me. He shifts and pulls my hips up with one hand, whilst pinning me down by the back of my neck with the other, pressing my cheek into the mattress. I grit my teeth and dig my nails into the mattress, my temper bubbling just below the surface.

"I suggest you don't pin me down like a bitch you're about to hump," I growl.

He laughs. "You seem to think you have some control here." His palm traces the length of my spine, before cupping my arse cheek and dragging his fingers over my crack. I flinch, because I'm not sure I trust him, and really, what can I do about it right now? His fingers work beneath the pathetic scrap of lace covering my pussy, and then he yanks it, tearing the material and leaving me completely exposed to him.

My heartbeat skitters, pounding against my eardrums loudly. "You're fucking beautiful," he rumbles, the growl in his voice making the compliment sound more like a curse. I'm sure he's going to fuck me, I'm practically shaking in anticipation, and then his grasp leaves my neck and the stubble of his jaw brushes against the back of my thigh. Hands grip my thighs, spreading me wide before he swipes his tongue over my pussy. Oh my fucking god. I shove my own fist in my mouth to stop from screaming out, but holy shit, that feels amazing. A low chuckle leaves his lips before he spreads me wider and thrusts his tongue inside me. A choked moan leaves my lips as my pussy quivers around him. His fingers dig into my skin hard enough that I can feel his nails biting into me. The more I squirm, the harder he presses his face into my pussy, until I'm pushing back against him, craving more. I want him deeper, until he's buried inside me. A low growl makes its way up his throat, sending a rush of hot breath over me. Desperation is eating away at me, and I roll my hips back, fucking his face like a wanton whore. He huffs a laugh before pulling away, sliding his hands up my thighs until he's gripping my arse. His fingers tighten, spreading my cheeks and making me tense. Hot breath blows over my crack, and I can't help but tremble even as my heart beats like a hummingbird's wings, the anticipation mixing with a hint of worry as the control freak in me raises its head.

I don't have time to think about it as his tongue swipes over my arsehole, making me gasp in shock. "Fuck, your arse is amazing," he rumbles, before pressing his tongue against my hole again. I shouldn't like it, but fuck, it's just so filthy dirty, so uninhibited. He presses his tongue inside me, at the same time as he slams two fingers into my pussy. It's a complete sensory overload: his tongue in my arse, his fingers in my pussy, the domination, the possession. *Fuck.* My body tightens, every muscle trembling as he fucks me with his tongue and fingers. My hips roll against him of their own violation, and he groans as he spreads his fingers inside me. *Oh, fuck.* My core tightens, everything focusing on one point before it explodes outwards, rippling over my muscles in a wave of pure pleasure that seems to roll on and on until I'm practically begging him to stop. I collapse face first on the bed, my chest heaving as I try to catch my breath. My legs are still shaking, and my pussy is so wet I can feel it down my thighs. I can't even find it in me to be ashamed. I roll over onto my back, looking up at him. He stands there, naked, every muscle beautifully tense. He looks like he was sculpted out of stone for the sole purpose of destroying women the world over. His fingers are wrapped tightly around his cock, and the muscles in his forearm pop with the effort of stroking the length of it.

I drag my eyes over his chiselled abs, his perfectly defined chest, his corded neck muscles, the firm set of his jaw, before I meet his gaze. I stare into those dark depths, watching as something flashes, something so very far removed from the rigid control I'm used to witnessing in him.

I sit up and crook a finger at him. He kneels on the bed and I push my hand against his chest, taking him off guard and shoving him onto his back. An amused smirk pulls at his lips as he watches me swing my leg over his body. I just want to feel his cock pressing against me so fucking badly. I slide my pussy over his cock slowly, feeling every hard inch of him. He swallows hard and his lips part as his eyes become hooded behind that dark mask. He grasps what is left of my dress, hanging uselessly around my waist and yanks the material, shredding it completely before discarding it somewhere beyond the bed. His warm palm presses against my stomach, making its way up to my breast and squeezing it roughly.

I trail my hand over his abs, fisting his thick cock, my fingers barely wrapping all the way around. I take a condom from the bowl on the bedside table and roll it over his length. His chest heaves unevenly and very muscle in his body stands rigid as I rise over him, then slowly lower into his cock. His patience is fleeting though, and he grips my hips, forcing me down on him hard. There's a small bite of pain as my pussy stretches around him, adjusting to his size.

"Fuck, Georgia." I didn't like him saying my name only moments ago, but now I very much like it. "I've thought about this tight pussy day and night since I laid eyes on you." That shouldn't be hot. But it's Landon, and having his attention is like a hit all of its own. I tighten my pelvic muscles, clenching around him and dragging a guttural groan from his throat. I'm burning up, my skin tingling. This is already better than any sex I've ever had, and I haven't even moved yet.

I roll my hips over him and holy shit, he feels so good, reaching parts of me no one else ever has. His fingers dig into my hips, pulling me down, forcing me to take every hard inch of him. My clit rubs over his abs which tense and flex with every movement, sending sparks of electricity flying through me.

"Ride me, kitten" he commands, making me roll my hips faster and faster. He's beautiful beneath me, all hard muscles and sweat slicked tanned skin. If I thought getting on top was going to make him the bottom, I was so wrong. His grip is like iron as he manipulates my body, but god, he does it so well. I'm like a puppet on his strings. It's not long though before he's done laying on his back. I let out a little squeak as he flips me over, pinning my hands above my head. He teases his lips over my neck, sinking his teeth into my skin as he pulls out of me and then slams back in. My mouth falls open on a silent scream as he brutally fucks me, pushing me right up to the pain-pleasure line with every thrust.

"Take it."

A bead of sweat rolls down the column of his throat and between his pecs before it drops onto my own sweat slicked skin. He grabs my knees and shoves them to my chest and it's like he just grew another inch of cock.

He leans back and stares at the point where his dick disappears inside me. There's something intoxicating in the intensity of it all, in the flexing of that beautiful body, the possession in his gaze as he stares at us both joined.

Those dark eyes meet mine, the mask surrounding them making him seem sinister and forbidden. "You're going to come on my cock and scream my fucking name, Georgia." I want to tell him to fuck off, that I won't, but for the first time in my life, I think I might have met my match.

His fingers wrap around my throat as he fucks me faster, using the grip for leverage. My airway restricts and adrenaline fires through my veins like sweet poison, sending me over the precipice of a cliff, the height of which seems endless. My core tightens and heat rips over me as the orgasm tears through me. My pussy clamps down on his dick and I cry out, clawing at his arm as my vision blurs. A guttural roar leaves his lips, his grip tightening further as he throws his head back. His thrusts become stiff and disjointed as he comes inside me, and all the while, my vision starts to blacken at the edges.

He collapses on top of me, his grip releasing and allowing me my first lungful of air in what feels like minutes. I close my eyes, trying to catch my breath, coming back down to earth. Our slick bodies slide against each other and I honestly can't remember ever being fucked that hard.

"Next time, I'm going to fuck that tight arse of yours, kitten," he says, placing one last drugging kiss against my lips before he pushes off me. His smug grin brings me down from my sex haze.

"There won't be a next time."

He gets dressed before he casually strolls over to the bed and stands over me, his eyes tracing the lines of my naked body. "We'll see."

I open my mouth to deny it but he presses his lips to mine, invading my mouth with his tongue. When he pulls away I can't remember what I was arguing about. "Remember Kitten, you asked for this. I'm not done with you yet."

And then he turns around and walks out of the room, leaving me naked and speechless on the bed. I glance at my shredded dress on the floor. Arsehole.

15

MONDAY MORNING, I'm so anxious about the prospect of seeing Landon in the office that I'm up and in the gym by six o'clock. I run until my legs are numb and sweat coats my entire body. Running usually clears my mind, but not today. My weekend involved a post Landon crisis and some tough love from Quinn. Her advice being, either bang him again, quit or carry on as though nothing happened, but quit bitching about it. She doesn't understand though. I let him control me. I let him dominate me. Had we walked in that club, and I'd controlled him, it would be completely different. I'd have used him. Done. Back to normal. But somehow I feel used, and that's an issue I can't get past.

When I get to work, I tap my foot anxiously, waiting for the lift to make its way to the top of the building. When I step off, I don't even spare a glance at Susan. I'm just going to go in, hand my resignation to Angus and walk out. Of course I'll work a month's notice. I'll have to, those are the terms of my contract. And seeing as I'm not willing to admit to Angus the real reason for me leaving, it's an amicable termination of contract and therefore the terms must be adhered to. At least Landon will know where I stand though. It was a mistake.

My stomach churns horribly as I step into the office. Landon is nowhere to be seen and I release the breath I'd been holding as I walk over to his empty desk and pop the envelope in the centre. I pause for a second, my eyes locked on the white paper as I swallow hard. I like Angus. I like this job. I don't want to leave, but it's for the best. My life has always been black and white, clear-cut, simple and with a sole focus in mind. Now Landon has suddenly painted it in a kaleidoscope of greys in the space of two short weeks. He's a black mark on my otherwise unblemished record and the fact that I allowed that all for the sake of lust...it makes me sick. So you see I need to leave, I have to get away from him, away from this, because despite what I previously thought, I'm not stupid enough to think that we can simply forget about it. I certainly can't.

I force myself to turn around and walk out. I go back to my office, and start work for the day, waiting anxiously for the phone to ring, and for Angus to call me up to his office.

Eva bustles in and out, flashing nervous glances at me and continuously asking if I'm okay. I shoo her away every time, sending her on menial tasks that really don't need doing. Of course, she knows that and it makes her more suspicious. I'm not a person that makes friends easily, but I like Eva so I make every effort not to be a bitch, and trust me, it doesn't come easy.

It's nearly midday when my office door bursts open and Landon walks in without knocking, closing and locking the door behind him. The sound of the lock clicking into place seems to reverberate around the room far more loudly than it should.

He turns to face me, placing his hands on his hips as he

tilts his face down, focusing on the ground. His usually immaculate image is ruffled this morning. His jacket and tie are missing and the sleeves of his shirt are rolled up, exposing his thick forearms. His hair is disheveled as though he's been dragging his hands though it all morning. Taking a shaky breath, I remember what it felt like to have my fingers in his hair, his cock inside me, his tongue on me, his body against mine. My mind replays the image of him moving beneath me, his biceps tensing as he forced me down on him, his abs rolling with every thrust. I squeeze my thighs together as my underwear becomes uncomfortably wet. I fight the urge to fan myself as a hot flush works over my skin. And the entire time he just stands there, refusing to look at me. Yep, I definitely need to leave. I wait, my heart beating so loudly I'm sure he can hear it in the deafening silence of the room.

"Why?" he asks, lifting his gaze to mine, making me squirm under his scrutiny. I clench my fists under the desk, letting my nails bite into the palms of my hands in an attempt to pull my mind out of the damn gutter.

"You know why," I breathe. I can't even speak properly.

He narrows his eyes as he takes slow strides towards the desk. Then leans over it, bracing his palms against the wood. I sit back, trying to put as much space as possible between us. A smirk takes over his face, but it's not the usual sexy smirk, this one is twisted with something dark and hard. "Did I miss something?" he asks. I frown in confusion. "Because the last I checked, you were the one who invited me to your secret sex club, and now you're running." He shakes his head. "I thought you could separate the two, Georgia." Unease crawls over me at the hint of disappointment in his voice. Wait, what? Why the fuck do I give a shit what he thinks? This is about me and my career.

I fix my expression into a steely mask and push up from my chair, stepping closer to him until the desk bumps the front of my thighs. "I'm not running. I'm doing what's best for my career."

"I don't care if you go. There are a hundred brokers ready to take your place, but Angus already thinks I fucked you. He's going to bitch like a motherfucker."

I glare at him. "Why would he think that? What did you say?"

He tilts his head to the side. "It might have something to do with the fact that most days you look at me like you want to fuck me and slit my throat at the same time." *Because I fucking do.*

"I do not look at you like I want to fuck you." I try to keep my voice low. Eva is a nosy bitch, and totally on team 'fuck Landon', so she probably has her ear pressed to the door right now. "See, this is why I'm leaving," I say, stabbing my finger into the desk and scowling at him.

"Why are you whispering?" He brings his face even closer to me.

I stand upright again, throwing my hands in the air. "Oh, I don't know, perhaps because I don't want the entire office to know that I fucked the boss," I hiss under my breath.

He rolls his eyes, and moves around the desk. I mirror his action, putting more space between us as he tries to close it. Eventually I end up on the other side in a stand off, while he stands in front of my chair, an incredulous look on his face.

"Really?" He drags a hand over the stubble on his face. "You invited me to that club knowing that you would have to walk back in here afterwards. What changed?" I shake my head and squeeze my eyes shut, trying to drag my scrambled thoughts into some sort of order. I don't hear him move, until his chest brushes against my arm. My eyes flash open and I glance at him. "What changed?" he asks again, softer this time.

My eyes meet his, and there's a beat of silence, an anxious pause that seems to stretch between us. "I fucked up."

He leans in close to my side that his lips are at my ear, hot breath washing over my neck. "You lost control," he breathes. "You liked my fingers around your throat, and my cock buried in your pussy." Heat washes over me, and I know my face is probably burning. Not because of his words, but because of where he's saying them. "And now you're panicking." God, he's right. He's completely right. I was stupid to think that I would ever have even an ounce of control when it comes to this man.

"Like I said, I fucked up." I turn my face until our lips are almost touching. "Rule number one: Never fuck the boss."

His lips twitch, forming a wry smile. "In this office, I'm your boss, but in that club I'm no one, remember? Just a guy in a mask."

Just a guy in a mask. If only that were the case. Landon Banks could never be 'just' anything no matter how hard he tries. I tear my gaze from his and focus on the London skyline, each sky scraper reflected in the windows of the next, like a giant house of mirrors. "It's really that simple for you?" I ask, turning to him once more. The sexual tension that I've become so used to crackles between us like a living thing. I don't miss the way his eyes flick to my lips.

"It's that simple." He steps back and holds his hands up in a surrendering gesture. "See, no need to leave."

I press my lips together, thinking the situation over in my mind. I go backwards and forwards while he watches me the entire time, waiting patiently for my response. "I need to think it over."

He says nothing as he takes a piece of paper from his jacket pocket and puts it on the desk in front of me. I pick it up, unfolding it and reading over my own words, my resignation.

"Meet me at The Mayfair Club tonight," he says. "Don't make any decisions until then."

This is stupid. I shouldn't be giving him any more chances to burrow under my skin. I think I'm strong enough to fight him but I'm clearly not. There's a reason I fucked him in the first place. I didn't make that decision lightly. If I'm honest, I'm running because I don't trust myself around him. Landon is a force to be reckoned with, and his brand of attack is one my hormones don't seem to be able to fight. I have never had a weakness in my life, but it seems he's it. I should hand him back my resignation and tell him to fuck off. *Should* being the key word.

"What time?" I find myself saying.

16

I'm a little drunk when I descend the stairs at The Mayfair bar. I've been at Rouge with Quinn for the last two hours, listening to her guess every conceivable reason as to why he's asked me here.

I glance around the bar, but I can't see Landon, he must not be here yet. I order a martini and a bag of Mexy. The bar maid gets to work making the drink before placing it and the tiny bag of white powder in front of me. I'm too drunk to speak to Landon right now. God knows I need every ounce of sensible thinking when I'm around that man.

I down the drink and then head to the bathroom. As soon as I snort the little line of white powder, the Mexy hits me, chasing away the drunken fog that's surrounding me and replacing it with a heightened awareness of everything around me. I drag a hand through my hair and swipe a new layer of lipstick over my lips before I leave the bathroom.

I spot Landon straight away sitting on a barstool, his elbow propped on the bar and a sexy smile on his lips as a brunette in a tight dress laughs at something he said. He's my boss, I should be indifferent to everything he does and yet I instantly wonder whether he would fuck her. I walk towards him, swinging my hips with every stride.

His gaze flicks over the woman's shoulder, tracking my progress towards him. I angle my body between him and the woman and place a hand on his chest. "You wanted to talk." I say, cocking a brow.

A smirk kicks up the corner of his lips. "It was nice meeting you," he says to the brunette. I can imagine the look of disappointment on her face, after all, who doesn't want to fuck Landon Banks?

He stands and wraps an arm around my waist, pulling me tightly into his side with a possessive jerk. He lowers his face to mine as he leads me away from the bar and my lungs freeze as his breath touches my cheek, his lips so painfully close.

"You're high," he comments dryly.

I focus ahead of me, refusing to look at him. "Last time I checked, you don't get a say in what I do in my spare time."

He ignores me and we stop at a door set back into the dark wall. I've never even noticed it before. It opens into a short hallway with another door at the end. He swipes a card over the metal box on the wall and a low buzz sounds before the door clicks open.

"Is this where you tell me you own this place?" I grumble.

"No, I have an exclusive membership." I step into the room beyond the door. It's a smaller version of the main bar, but more intimate. The tables are well spaced with sheer curtains pulled across the little corner booths.

"An exclusive membership in an already exclusive club?" I ask. I mean, really? He simply shrugs one shoulder as he takes a seat at the booth nestled into the corner. No one else is in here except for the bartender and the lack of people makes me nervous.

I sit across from him, leaning back against the seat and keeping my hands in my lap. He watches me like a predator looking for weakness. I wait for him to speak first, because he's the one who brought me here. The longer the silence stretches on, the more I fidget. Even when the waiter brings us drinks without us even ordering, he still doesn't speak. God, why does he make me so nervous?

He unbuttons his jacket and slips his hand inside, pulling a slim envelope from the inside pocket. He places it on the table and slides it in front of me before retracting his hand.

"What is this?" I ask, eyeing it suspiciously.

He clasps his hands together on the table in front of him. "Open it." His expression is hard as he stares at me, waiting.

I pick up the envelope and pull back the unsealed flap, sliding the single piece of paper out. My eyes skim over the first few lines and pop wide.

"A contract?" I ask, looking at him in disbelief. He nods. "Why? Is this some kind of joke?" I snap, my temper rising.

"No, no joke." He taps his index finger against his bottom lip. "I can't be professional with you, Georgia." It's a confession, a plea almost.

I freeze, unsure what to say to that.

"I know what it is to fuck you." My pulse leaps. "I know how good you taste, how perfect you sound when you come." Oh god, I can't breathe. I part my lips on a staggered breath and his eyes drop to my mouth. "And you want me, or you wouldn't feel the need to hand in your notice." I don't deny it. I can't. "So that leaves us at an impasse, a seemingly impossible situation."

I pick up my drink taking a heavy gulp that does nothing

to ease my dry throat or the heat in my veins. "So why not just let me leave?"

He leans in, his eyes locking with mine and darkening beneath the dim lighting. "One taste wasn't nearly enough, kitten."

I squeeze my thighs together, unable to tear my gaze from his. "I won't be your dirty office fuck."

He points to the paper in my hand. "This is a contract that outlines very specific details, boundaries as it were. The office is off limits." He drew up a contract to fuck? That's... I don't even know.

I skim over the document.

Agreement between Landon Banks (herein referred to as "The Primary") and Georgia Roberts (herein referred to as "The Secondary").

1. The Secondary shall adhere to her current terms of employment and treat the The Primary with the respect that should be afforded to her employer.

2. The Primary and Secondary will meet at agreed times at "Masque", and only within this establishment will sexual activity be permitted.

3. The Primary and secondary may not conduct in any sexual activity outside of "Masque".

4. Neither party may speak of their time within "Masque".

5. Neither party will discuss the terms of this contract.

6. Breach of this contract will result in immediate termination of the contract.

7. Should The Primary breach the terms of the

contract, then he will leave Redford and Banks London offices for the forseeable future.

8. This agreement in no way effects the employment or career of The Secondary.

9. This agreement will be ongoing until one or both parties declares it void.

There at the bottom is Landon's signature, with a space for mine and my name typed beneath the line.

"You want a contract to fuck?" I ask incredulously.

He leans forward, his eyes meeting mine. "I want to fuck you Georgia. So here it is, in black and white with clear lines, just the way you like it."

"You drew up a contract." I repeat. "Just so you could fuck me."

A wicked smile makes its way onto his face. "I promised you I'd fuck that sweet arse of yours." His voice is barely above a growl. "I keep my promises."

"And what if I want to fuck your sweet arse?" I ask, cocking a brow.

The smile that pulls at his lips is nothing short of sinful. "You can try."

I take a deep breath, because all joking, lusting and fucking aside, this is serious. If I sign this, I'm agreeing to something that I'm not sure I can control. I already feel like I'm in way over my head with him, and that's without the involvement of sex.

He picks up his glass of bourbon. "We both know how this goes. Either I fuck you or you quit."

"Are you blackmailing me now?"

"I'm simply stating fact. It will happen again because as much as you want to deny it, you can't help yourself." His gaze sweeps over me. "And neither can I." He's right. My tightly regimented world is in peril because of this man, but if there's a contract then the act of fucking him becomes regimented, with it's own set of rules. I can control this, and that control makes me feel safe, even if it is a false sense of security. Or maybe this is exactly what I need, to create a new set of rules to suit this particular situation.

"Do you have a pen?" I ask.

His expression remains stoic as he pulls a pen from his inside pocket, holding it out to me. I take it from him and place the paper on the table in front of me. I know this is all ridiculous and that this contract is in no way actually binding, but I feel like I'm signing my life away, whoring myself out to my boss. Maybe I want to be his whore? Shit, I don't even know what I want.

I place the pen to the paper and scrawl my signature on it, the black seeming to taint the crisp white space. He takes the paper from me before the ink is even dry and folds it up, placing it back in his pocket.

"Now what?" I ask.

"Now..." He slides out of the booth and stands, smoothing his hands down the front of his jacket. "We're going to Masque."

17

I STEP INTO MASQUE, unnecessarily conscious of Landon at my side. I'm convinced everyone is looking at us, like they know I just walked in with my boss. Of course they don't and no one gives a shit. There is no normal here, everything is its own brand of anything goes. I glance around but before I can take a step, I'm pulled into one of the little alcoves only three feet from the front door. It's covered by a floor to ceiling black satin curtain which falls into place behind us. The club is full of these little nooks and crannies, private, but still offering the thrill that comes with the possibility of being caught.

I don't know what I was expecting, but one minute I'm standing, the next Landon's hands are on my waist, lifting me and forcing me up against the wall. Any lingering doubts are completely extinguished under his touch, not gone, but certainly forgotten. I can think of nothing but him. My legs wrap around his hips and my hands around his neck, clinging to him for support. Hot breath caresses my throat before his lips press against the soft skin, skating a line up the side of my neck. My lungs feel too small, incapable of drawing sufficient air. His lips have been on my skin for mere seconds and I'm wet and desperate already. It's not just the fact that he's touching me, it's the lack of guilt. I feel like my signature on that contract has somehow freed me and as long as I'm inside these walls I can lust after Landon all I want. He wants me, and I want him, and here, in this club, that's all that matters.

I grab a handful of his hair, yanking his head back and forcing him to look at me. The black mask cloaks his eyes in shadow making them seem even darker than they already are. I brush my lips across his teasingly and bourbon laced breaths blow over my lips. His lips part and I suck his bottom lip into my mouth, biting down on it. He groans, fingers digging into my thighs. Lust ignites between us like an inferno, buzzing over my skin, stealing my breath.

"I need to fuck you," he growls against my throat.

God, and I need him to fuck me. His fingers slip away, allowing me to stand. I wish I knew why Landon effects me so much. God knows, he's usually the type of guy I hate, and I do hate him but you can't fight animal attraction. And this level of attraction is its own kind of rush, a little adrenaline kick to the soul. In a world where professionalism and image is everything, Landon is my own personal rebellion.

He pushes through the thin curtain and I follow him, allowing him to lead me up the stairs.

Once inside the room, he closes the door behind me and starts removing his cuff links, placing them on a little side table with a heavy clink. His calm manner has my heart beating so loudly I'm sure he must be able to hear me.

He removes his shirt, then sits on the edge of the bed, methodically removing his shoes, socks and trousers. Everything about him is controlled, almost unshakeable.

We'll see. I lower the zip on my dress and slide it down

my arms before I step out of the material. My bra goes next and his gaze slowly lifts, playing over every line and curve of my body clad in red lace underwear and high heels. Nothing else.

"You're dangerous, kitten."

I swing a leg over his thighs, and lower myself onto his lap, straddling him. His muscular chest rises and falls beneath my palm, his breaths heavy. Landon is all man, his body a work of art, sculpted and honed to perfection, and I want to possess him, for him to possess me. His cock presses against me, rock hard and insistent.

"Do you want me, Landon?"

I allow my fingertips to trace every bump and dip of his abs before slipping below the waistband of his boxers.

"More than my next fucking breath." His eyes darken as I grip his cock, teeth clenched as I work my hand over him, gripping tightly. I move lower, cupping his balls, rolling them in my hand. His breathing becomes ragged and he throws his head back on a low groan. Watching a man come apart is always satisfying, but watching a man like Landon come apart is a whole other level. Sex is power, and this, with him, is the pinnacle.

I scratch my nails over the stubble of his face and press my lips to his, teasing caresses and gentle nips that have him tensing beneath me. The kiss is short lived before he grabs me and launches me. I land on my back on the mattress, the air leaving my lungs in a rush.

"You're playing with fire, Georgia." His fingers hook into my underwear, dragging them down my legs and tossing them to the side before he flips me over onto my front and wrenches my hips up until I'm braced on my elbows with my arse in the air. I feel exposed and vulnerable, possessed in the most exciting way. My breaths become erratic as I glance over my shoulder at him. Adrenaline floods my system, that little spark of excitement igniting in my chest.

Fingers trail up my spine and I shiver, my skin breaking out in goose bumps. His lips follow the path of his fingers and I moan when his tongue swipes across the back of my neck. Landon is an artist in anticipation. He has me desperate, hanging on by a thread, feeling as though I may scream if he doesn't touch me, and just when I settle into his gentle touches, he snaps, his touch becoming bruising and forceful. It turns me on so much I can barely see straight.

He grips my jaw, twisting my head back until he has access to my lips. His tongue traces the seam of my mouth as his cock presses against me, slowly pushing inside me inch by torturous inch. I choke out a moan as he slides deep inside me. I can taste his ragged breaths on my tongue as he pauses, the fingers around my jaw tightening. He starts to move, hips rolling as a string of groans fall from his lips. I can't move with the grip he has on my face, my head wrenched back and my back bowed, allowing him to fuck me so deep that it just rides the pleasure pain barrier.

"Fuck!" His grip shifts to the back of my neck, forcing my cheek into the mattress as he begins hammering into me.It's absolute domination, and I shouldn't like a thing about it, but I crave more.

I'm clutching handfuls of the sheets and moaning his name like a man prayer as sweat coats my body. His hand leaves my neck and tracks down my spine, over the crack of my arse. His touch is gentle, teasing, even as he fucks me like he wants to climb inside me.

I hear him spit and feel warm liquid trailing down my crack. My breath hitches. He's so fucking dirty and I want every sordid bit of it. .

"I promised you I'd take this sweet arse, kitten." He says

through labored breaths. A finger presses against me *there*, and I tense.

He lets out a low chuckle. "Relax." His thrusts slow and I take a deep breath, pressing my forehead against the mattress. Have I had a finger in my arse before? Well yeah, who hasn't? But when he's putting a finger in my arse while threatening me with the monster he keeps in his pants, it's not reassuring. He works his finger in my arse while continuing his rhythmic fucking of my pussy. Slowly he picks up the pace and damn, the man can work magic. It feels so good. When I'm groaning and biting down on my own arm he slides another finger in, stretching me. Shit.

And then he goes to town fucking me with everything he has, his dick buried in my pussy while his fingers work in and out of my arse. Everything builds, teetering on a precipice that feels like it may either kill me, or make me come harder than I ever have in my life, and I do. I fall, tumbling through wave after wave of orgasm until I'm screaming his name. He keeps fucking me until I beg him to stop and he pulls out. I collapse face down on the mattress shaking and twitching, my muscles completely limp. His hands never leave my hips, keeping me in position even as I struggle to catch a full breath.

He rubs his dick along my arse crack, but I'm too fucked to even move or really acknowledge it. His fingers dig into my arse cheeks, spreading them wide before he spits on me again, using his dick to spread the moisture that's covering my pussy all over my arse. He's going to fuck me there, and it's not something I've ever done, but for some reason I want to let him. I can't even justify it to myself, but I want his brand of filth and dominance.

I push up onto my elbows and lock them, bracing for it. "Just relax, kitten."

And I am relaxed, which was well played on his part. He presses against me, and it feels a damn site bigger than his fingers. "Relax." He repeats.

He pushes past the ring of muscle and it burns like a bitch. I bite my lip as he pushes on, sliding further and further inside me. Okay, now I feel a bit sorry for Apollo. I've never been this gentle with him.

There's pressure and pain, but as soon as he's inside me he stops. I can feel his hands trembling on my hips. "Jesus, fuck." He presses his lips into my back. "Your arse is so fucking tight. So perfect."

The longer he stays there the more I relax, and when he starts to move, I'm biting my lip for entirely different reasons. His movements are slow and accompanied by a string of groans.

I glance over my shoulder watching the way his body pops with restraint, the way the corded muscles of his neck stand out as he throws his head back. I want him to break the same way he breaks me. I want him to cross the point of no return where an orgasm becomes so much more, so I make him.

"Come inside me, Landon. I want you to come in my arse." His head snaps forward, his eyes meeting mine, black, bottomless, feral. His hips move faster, driving into me. It takes seconds for him to shatter, coming hard and shouting my name like a curse, over and over. When he's done he pulls out of me, falling on his back and closing his eyes as his sweat slick chest heaves.

I just let Landon take something I never thought I'd be willing to give. I've fucked him twice and I feel owned and branded in every possible way. We may have a contract to fuck, but right now it feels like I just signed away the deed to my body.

18

I WAS anxious to see how mine and Landon's little agreement would actually pan out when we got back in the office, but it's been fine, or rather he's been fine. It's been two weeks and he's been nothing but professional, dare I say it almost indifferent, just as he promised. That burning lust I felt for him however has only intensified, and it makes me hate him. I hate that he compromises me. I hate that I let him fuck me. I hate that I like him controlling me. I hate that I want him, even while hating him. I hate it! As a result, I do my utmost to ignore him in the office.

We're sitting in another meeting with a new client. We're in Oblix, on the thirty second floor of the Shard, looking over London bridge. We did the sociable bullshit required with a new client, you know, make them feel as if we're friends, genuinely invested in their future. Of course, we are, but it sure as shit isn't because we're just such nice people. We're invested because his money makes us money and more importantly my bonus. I'm half listening to the guy talk about his current investments, and I should be listening, focusing, doing my job to the best of my ability, but I'm not. My eyes track the movement of Landon's arm as he brings it up to rest his elbow on the table. His bicep strains against the material of his shirt as he drags his index finger over his bottom lip.

"Ms. Roberts." I snap out of my daze and look up at Mr. Morris, his expression expectant. *Shit.* I can feel Landon's eyes burning a hole in the side of my face, and I try to stop the blush from creeping into my cheeks, of course that just makes it worse. Thank god for Double Wear foundation.

Landon clears his throat. "Georgia works very closely with all our major companies. She can recommend the most dependable ones to you. I'm sure she can draw up a proposal..."

"Yes, of course. I'll draw up a detailed proposal with profit and loss figures for the last five years, as well as future forecasting and risk evaluation." I throw in a smile, hoping that he doesn't notice that I wasn't listening to a word he said.

He smiles back, clearly satisfied. Thank god. "Well then I look forward to seeing what you come up with." He says.

We stand up, shake hands, exchange pleasantries, all that bullshit, and then I'm heading for the door, refusing to look back at Landon. This is how it is with us, how it has to be when we're at work. Now if only I could tame my hormones and force my mind to separate work and play with a big black line, that would be great. It's not helped by the fact that he looks like a walking sex icon at all times. Seriously, can't he just have a bad day occasionally?

I push through the doors and into the hallway where the bank of elevators are. I hear the door creak open behind me as I slam my hand on the button for the lift. I feel him behind me without even looking, and when the lift arrives I step inside, pulling my phone out and focusing on my screen. I don't even see what's in front of me, because all my attention is centered on him. That familiar pressure on my chest builds the longer I stand in the small space with him, and I lean against the side of the small metal box.

"You stalled." He says quietly.

"Thanks for your help." I reply coldly, attempting to brush off my obvious distraction. As soon as the doors open, I'm walking again, trying to put some distance between us, of course he's well over six foot, his long legs easily keeping up with me. He grabs my upper arm, yanking me sideways so violently that I stumble into him, wobbling on my heels and falling against his chest. "What the hell?" I snap, shoving my hands against his hard chest and pushing away from him.

We're still on the street, but pulled into an alcove set into the brick work of the building. I glance nervously around at the people passing by, worried that someone might recognise us.

"What happened to professional?" He says.

I frown. "What?"

"It states in the contract that we are to be professional with one another." He cocks a dark eyebrow at me.

"I am being professional. You're the one who just manhandled me."

"You really think this ice queen act of yours is professional?" He drags a hand over his face.

I clench my jaw, biting back the 'fuck you' that's on the tip of my tongue. It's the comment every career woman hates: ice queen, bitch, man hater. This is the shit I avoid like the plague, painting fake smiles on my face rather than giving them the middle finger. I'm already aggravated by him, but now I'm just mad.

"I am simply doing my job. Don't like it, then fire me." I spit.

He steps closer and I move back, until the rough brick wall hits my back, scratching at the material of my dress. He steps even closer, until he's pressed against me and my nose is barely an inch from the skin of his throat. I slam my eyes closed as his scent surrounds me, making me want to sigh in relief. I shiver when his breath blows over my scalp.

"I have no intention of firing you, Georgia." He says, his deep voice reverberating through my body, caressing my name. My mind blinks like a film reel, images of Landon fucking me, licking me, kissing me, flashing one after the other. I gasp, and my hand flies to his chest again, slipping beneath the lapel of his jacket and pressing against the warm cotton of his shirt. He shifts, and I feel his fingers gently grip my chin, tilting my face up to his.

"Look at me." He says under his breath.

I inhale a shaky breath and even though I know it's a bad idea I open my eyes, meeting his dark gaze. Everything around us stops, as though we're completely invisible, caught in our own little bubble. His grip on my chin slips and he drags his thumb across my bottom lip until he's cupping my cheek. My heart hammers in my chest, thrumming in my ears like a drum. I spot the flash of desire in his eyes a second before he kisses me. His lips press against mine almost reverently, teasing, tentative as though he's unsure of his actions. I try to remember why this shouldn't be happening, but he renders me stupid, incapable of thinking. My hand moves up his chest, until I'm gripping the back of his neck, pulling him down to me while I push up onto my tip toes, desperate to get closer to him. His tongue swipes across my lower lip and I part my lips, allowing him in. I kiss him until I'm drowning in him, until he grips my face with both hands and physically breaks our connection. When I open my eyes, the look on his face is animalistic, as though he's on the edge of snapping. We remain like that for a second, and it seems as though he's warring with himself, the indecision written all over his face.

"Go, Georgia." He orders, moving back a step and dropping his gaze to the floor. He rubs a hand over his mouth. "Take the car. I'll see you tonight." And then he turns around and walks in the opposite direction, leaving me standing there

I turn and walk as fast as I can across the street, hopping in the waiting town car. So much for our supposed clear lines. I'm not sure that either of us really has any control of this.

I take the car to one of the local bars just around the corner from Quinn's office. It's seven, so I'm deeming this appropriate drinking time. I shoot Quinn a text telling her to meet me here.

Fifteen minutes later she walks in, glancing around the place and looking like she just sniffed dog shit.

"Okay, why the fuck are we here?" She asks.

"To get drunk." Granted the dive bar isn't exactly our normal scene and Quinn looks laughably out of place in her Armani suit.

"Can't we do that somewhere else?"

I push the Cosmopolitan I ordered for her in front of her. "Nope. I don't need to be seen drunk." None of our social circle are likely to walk in here.

"Fine. What are we drinking to?"

"To fucking up." I lift my half glass of vodka, because I

skipped the attempt at class and went straight to drunken mess.

She rolls her eyes as we clink glasses. "What happened?"

"Landon accused me of being unprofessional." Her eyebrows shoot up. "Then he kissed me on the street and I pretty much assaulted him back."

She flashes me a disapproving look. "If you can't keep that dog on a leash then you need to cut him loose."

I snort. "You have met Landon Banks, right? That man can't be leashed."

She shrugs. "You know what you should do, George. You don't need me to tell you."

I do, but for some reason, when it comes to him, I'm rendered incapable of thinking past my fucking vagina. Does that make me weak for allowing him to consume me, or strong for taking what I want? Stupid. It makes me stupid for even getting in this, let alone staying in it. Landon is not a dog, he's a fucking wolf. And I'm the tigress who turns into a kitten as soon as I'm near him. Fuck him. I hate him.

The longer I think about it, the angrier I get. Landon Banks is a fucking arsehole.

19

When I get to Masque I head straight up the stairs. I'm pissed off, like really pissed off...and tipsy. I keep replaying that kiss in my head over and over, and each time it makes me a little more indignant. So much for his contract. I should declare it void and tell him to fuck off back to Dubai. That would be best for both of us!

His tie is wrapped around the door of room 12, the same room we always use. I push the door open and slip inside, closing it behind me.

Landon is standing in the middle of the room, the sleeves of his shirt rolled up past his forearms and his top few shirt buttons undone. He watches me as I push away from the door and storm towards him. Before I even have a chance to think it through I swing my arm back and slap him. Hard. The clap of my palm meeting his face rings out around the room and his head snaps to the side.

When he swings his gaze back to me, I take a wary step back. "Georgia." He growls, ripping his mask off. Every natural instinct is telling me I should run right about now, but anger wins out.

"Fuck you, Landon!"

His eyes flash dangerously and then he's barreling towards me. I back up a couple of steps and his hand flies to my throat as he continues to press me. I stumble back into the wall, and he slams me against it by my neck, crushing my shoulder blades into the plaster.

He brings his face close to mine and I can see a muscle twitching in his jaw as his finger tips flinch into the skin of my throat. "I will tell you once. Don't ever fucking hit me."

I wrap my hand around his wrist, squeezing tight enough that my nails cut into his skin. "Get your fucking hand off me." I grate.

He makes a show of slamming me back against the wall again and tightening his grip. "What the fuck is wrong with you?"

I laugh. "You! *Go Georgia*." I mimic his voice. "You tell me I'm unprofessional..."

He cocks a brow. "So that's what this is about."

"...and then you kiss me. In the middle of the fucking street, Landon!" My nails are screaming as they bend back against his skin. Finally, he releases me, but his body remains pressed against mine. "The contract was there for a reason, not just so you could get between my legs."

His lips pull into an infuriating smirk. "Kitten, we both know the contract was just an excuse for you to let me between your legs." *Arsehole. Fucking arsehole.*

I shove my hands against his chest, but it barely moves him. "I'm done."

He thrusts a hand in my hair and wrenches my head back, bringing his lips to my ear. "You kissed me back, kitten. I had to stop you before you started humping my leg. So don't preach to me."

I open my mouth to say something, but he slams his

mouth over mine. I force myself not to kiss him back, but he keeps going, forcing his tongue inside my mouth until I can't help myself. When it comes to him I don't seem to be able to. Ever. Even if everything I've worked for is at stake.

"It won't happen again." He murmurs against my lips.

It's not an apology, but it's enough. Enough to make me just a little less indignant, and enough that when I give in and press my lips to his it doesn't dent my pride.

An hour later I leave Masque after a serious round of hate fucking. I didn't think it was possible to hate someone while you're fucking them, and to hate the fact that you're fucking them, but be so consumed by them in that moment that it over-rides mere hatred. Apparently it is. With him it is, because no matter how many times I want to stop, I can't. He's become a fix, a strange sort of salvation.

If I'm honest, I don't hate him, I hate the person he turns me into. And it's easier to hate him than admit that he's so far under my skin I can't seem to dig him out.

20

Eva bustles into my office on Friday morning, placing a Starbucks cup in front of me. "Chai Latte." She says as she starts picking up documents and filing things away.

"I need that in a minute." I tell her.

"Well then you can get it out of the filing cabinet in a minute." She replies, completely ignoring me.

"You have issues."

"Yes, my messy boss."

"I am not messy!" I say indignantly. "Jesus, you should see Landon's desk."

She turns on her heel, lifting one perfectly plucked brow at me. "I wouldn't know. I'm not as close to the big boss as you are." I narrow my eyes at her and pick up the coffee, saying nothing. "Don't tell me some of those morning meetings don't involve a quickie."

"My meetings are with Angus, so no."

"Oooh, but you're not denying the idea of a quickie with Landon. Good to know." She smiles smugly and heads back out to her desk. "Oh." She pauses. "I forgot, he asked me to give you this." She turns around, pressing her lips together, trying to suppress a smile.

I frown as I take the envelope from her outstretched hand. She walks out of the room with a little spring in her step. She knows. Eva has some freaky intuition for pretty much anything, and if the chemistry between Landon and I is even half obvious to anyone else, then yeah, she knows. I refuse to confirm her suspicions though.

I open the envelope and scrawled over thick letter headed paper is Landon's handwriting.

Tonight. 10.30pm.

L

A text would have sufficed.

I open the door to room 12 and close it behind me.

I narrow my eyes at the figure sitting on the edge of the bed. It's not Landon.

"Apollo." I say, tilting my head to the side curiously. I glance around the room quickly and can't see Landon.

Apollo smiles that mischievous smile of his. "Did you miss me?" He asks.

I take slow steps towards him, crossing one leg over the other as I walk. "Hmm, shouldn't I be asking you that?" The closer I get to him the more the room opens out and my eyes finally fall on Landon sitting in a chair in the corner, his face cloaked in shadow. His ankle is propped on the other knee and his hands are resting casually along the arms of the leather chair. The shirt he's wearing is unbuttoned, show-casing tanned skin over rippling abs.

I swing my gaze back to Apollo and a slow smile pulls at my lips. "I always miss you." He winks.

I raise my eyebrow and turn away from him, walking

towards Landon. He remains completely still as he watches me walk towards him. I bend over, gripping his bare forearms beneath his rolled up shirt sleeves.

"You brought me a present?" I say quietly, my lips barely an inch from his.

He slowly snakes his hand up the back of my neck, fisting my hair as he presses his lips over mine. I try to deepen the kiss but his grip tightens, restraining me and sending a flash of pain over my scalp.

"I did." The second time I met him here after I signed the contract, he met me at the bar where I was talking to Apollo. As far as I know it's the only time he's seen him, and yet he went out of his way to seek him out. For this. For me.

He pushes to his feet. His hand is still buried in my hair, my face forcibly tilted up to his, my body pressed to his. When he steps forward, he forces me back with him.

"Move." Landon barks and I hear the bed creak before the mattress hits the back of my knees and I'm shoved back onto it. Landon towers over me, his gaze flicking off to the side where I can see Apollo lingering in my periphery.

"Feel free to watch this part." He rumbles and it takes me a second to realize that he's not talking to me. Apollo steps back out of view and it's like watching a pup bow down to the alpha. I've always found Apollo attractive but he suddenly seems so inferior. I watch Landon approach, shrugging the shirt off his shoulders as he walks. His face is serious, the teasing playful side of him nowhere to be seen. He wears that crippling power of his like armour, his body bristling effortlessly with it, and it makes me want to both recoil and throw myself at him at the same time.

I catch sight of Apollo moving into the chair in the corner. I've never been an exhibitionist. The idea of being watched has never done anything for me, but it's kind of hot.

He drops into a crouch, grabbing my knee's and dragging me to the edge of the bed whilst forcing my legs apart. He looks up at me, our eyes locking and that familiar electricity sparking between us. His hands slowly skate up my thighs, pushing the material of my dress higher and higher until my lace thong is exposed. One hand drops between my legs, his fingers slipping beneath the lace and brushing over my pussy. He touches me like it's his right, as though he can do what he wants with me. And truthfully, his touch renders me weak, any morals or thoughts of pride disappear and all I can think about is the next caress of his fingers, the brush of his lips over mine.

He thrusts two fingers inside me, watching intently as I buck and writhe under the sudden onslaught. He pulls out and thrusts back in and my eyes drift shut as I bite down on my bottom lip, stifling a moan.

"Look at me." He commands.

I open my eyes and watch as he lowers his face between my legs. He kisses the lace covering my clit and my pussy clenches around his fingers. His gaze darkens and he shoves my underwear to the side and drags his tongue over me so fucking slowly.

I whimper, fighting not to tear my eyes away because it's so intense. He starts circling his tongue over my clit whilst burying his fingers even deeper in my pussy. I hear a low groan from the corner, mingled with the sound of skin softly slapping.

When Landon spreads his fingers and swipes his tongue over my clit I throw my head back, a broken moan working its way up my throat. My arms give way until I'm flat on my back. I'm close, so fucking close, and then he pulls away and I want to cry out in frustration. He laughs as he rears up on his knees, grabbing my hips and flipping me over. This man seems to enjoy throwing me around like a rag doll.

"What are—" The material of my thong bites into my skin as he tears it from my body. Another pair of underwear ruined. I'm going to start billing him for them, I swear.

"Don't ask questions, kitten." He says as he wrenches my legs apart and slams two fingers back inside me. I choke on a groan, raking my nails over the satin sheets covering the bed. I'm soaking wet, my pussy throbbing with the need to come, yet still he teases, pulling his fingers out and smearing the moisture along my arse crack slowly. When he slides his fingers deep inside me and presses his thumb against my arsehole, I understand why. My mouth opens on a silent moan as his fingers thrust in and out of me. God, he's so fucking good with his hands. He waits until I'm moaning like a whore before he pushes against my arse again, slipping inside easily. I clench my teeth, gripping the sheets beneath me as he starts to fuck my pussy and my arse with his hand. This isn't him letting Apollo watch, this is him laying claim, filling me to the hilt to let me and Apollo know who owns this.

He works over me until I'm crying out, screaming desperately as the orgasm washes over me, him milking me for everything I'm worth as I come all over his fingers. When he's done, he slowly removes his fingers, dragging them over every sensitive nerve ending as he does. I roll onto my back, my chest heaving as I watch him stand, bending over me. His fingers clamp around my neck, pulling me up into a sitting position, forcing me to watch as he brings the two fingers that were just buried in my pussy to my mouth. He says nothing, but his eyes flash dangerously as he presses them against the seam of my lips. I open for him and he slides the digits inside, groaning when I wrap my tongue around them. I can taste myself on him, the saltiness mixing with the taste of his skin. I slowly pull my head back, sucking his fingers dry and releasing them with a little pop.

A pleased smile pulls at his lips and he strokes his thumb gently over the side of my neck before he releases me, standing and clicking his fingers at Apollo who is still sat there tugging on his dick. Yes, clicks at him like a fucking bus boy or some shit.

Apollo stands up, moving over to me. "Have fun, kitten." Landon says, winking at me before he steps back. I smile, pushing off the bed and going to my handbag. I take out The Destroyer. Landon watches me with genuine interest, his head tilted to the side as I strip out of my dress, leaving my bra on. I don't miss the way he steps in front of me, blocking Apollo's view as I step into the harness and fasten the straps.

"Jealous?" I ask, cocking an eyebrow.

"I don't share." He says.

"Hmm, maybe this exercise isn't for you then."

His lips pull up at one corner as he steps closer, but not close enough that he might risk getting poked with The Destroyer. "You can fuck him, but this…" He cups my crotch just below where the purple dick protrudes between my hip. "…is mine." He says, his voice low. I should tell him to go fuck himself and let Apollo fuck me on pure principle, but truthfully I don't want to fuck Apollo. Instead I just roll my eyes and put my hand on his bare chest, shoving him out of the way.

I approach Apollo and his eyes drop to the cock bobbing with every step. "No blow job?" He says, amusement lacing his voice.

"You know I don't suck cock."

"Worth a try." He says. "Is your friend going to partici-

pate or is he more of a voyeur?" He asks, smiling. Apollo is
not opposed to dudes. The guy just likes sex, anyway he can
get it. He's a raging slut. That's how I originally found him. I
saw him in Masque one night, bent over a dresser in the
hallway as you walk in, a guy balls deep inside him, while a
girl was sat on the dresser, legs spread wide and Apollo's
face in her pussy, eating her like it was his sole fucking
purpose in life. I found him hot because any guy who is that
comfortable that he will fuck, or be fucked any which way, is
attractive. The next week I approached him and thus our
strange arrangement came to be. He told me that first time
that I fuck better than a guy. I take that as a compliment.

"Bend over." I tell him. He knows the drill but I think he
likes it when I tell him what to do.

He gets up on the bed, crawling to the centre and getting
on all fours with his arse facing me. I slide up behind him
and pick up the bottle of lube off the side table, squeezing it
all over the purple silicone before throwing it to the side.
Landon has resumed his position in the chair, his ankle
propped on his knee in the exact same pose he had when I
walked in. His expression is completely indifferent as he
watches me shuffle forward an inch, fisting the silicone dick
and lining it up with Apollo's arse. I grip his hip, my fingers
slipping as I smear lube all over his skin. He flinches when I
press forward against his hole, and I'm not sure if it's
because he's scared of me, or if it's because that's just a
natural reaction to having something pressed against your
arsehole. Once he relaxes again, I push on until the tip
disappears inside him. He hums a low moan in the back of
his throat, dropping his head forward between his braced
arms as he takes more and more of the silicone toy.

My clit is throbbing as the straps rub over the the sensitive tissue. I slide the toy deep inside Apollo, until my thighs

touch the back of his and he lets out a choked groan. I don't look at Landon, instead I grip Apollo's hips hard enough that I can feel my nails bending back against his skin. I pull out of him and do what I do best: I fuck him. I fuck him until he's pushing back against me, begging for more as his hand strokes over his dick. I'm so consumed by the sight of him falling apart that I jump when I feel hands on my hips, a hot, bare chest at my back. Landon's lips hit my neck as his arms come around my waist, skating over my ribs and cupping my breasts in his big palms. He's naked and I can feel the smooth hardness of his cock pressing against my lower back. I throw my head back against his shoulder, allowing him access to my neck and breasts as I continue to fuck Apollo. The bed dips slightly behind me before his hands move to my hips, stilling my movements. He pushes a thigh between mine, forcing my legs apart. I grind against his thigh, seeking some friction from him.

"So fucking wet, kitten." He growls.

I can't form coherent words as he removes his thigh and presses his cock against my pussy, sliding between the strategically placed straps. He sinks balls deep inside me and I gasp, my fingers digging into Apollo. He hisses as my nails break the skin.

"Fuck him." Landon commands against my ear.

My legs are threatening to buckle, but I do as he says and begin rocking into Apollo. Each time I pull out of him, Landon thrusts forward, burying his cock impossibly deep. Apollo's groans intermingle with the sound of Landon's heavy breaths behind me. I'm so turned on, I can feel the moisture seeping down my thighs, soaking the straps between my legs.

I thrust harder, fucking both Apollo and myself more deeply. I cry out as he lets out a long groan, his arm jerking violently as he strokes his dick. He throws back his head, his body stiffening. I keep fucking him because I'm close and every time I move Landon's dick hits me in just the right spot. I slam my eyes closed, clinging to Apollo's hips for support, even as he trembles beneath me. Eventually Apollo pulls away, flinching as he does so. I would fall forward if it weren't for Landon's hands holding my hips firmly in place. Apollo rolls across the bed, laying on his back and panting heavily. A trail of his come is seeping into the satin sheets just inches from where my hands are splayed. Landon pulls out of me, and I want to cry out in frustration.

"Get out." He barks, his voice rich with the authority he wears so easily.

I lift my head and see Apollo scramble off the bed and gather his clothes before he exits the room. I roll over, my chest still heaving after the double fucking.

"That was mean." I tease.

He closes the distance between us, unclipping the straps on the toy and tossing it aside. He grips my thighs, wrenching them apart and forcing my knees to my chest. "You had your fun." He says, sliding between my legs.

"And you?" I ask. "Did you have fun?"

He leans over me, his body weight pushing my legs even harder against my chest. Thank fuck for yoga. "You're at your best when you're being a bitch." He rumbles against my lips. "Doesn't get much hotter than watching you own another guy with a ten-inch dick."

He pushes inside me and I bite down on my bottom lip. "You don't want my ten-inch dick?"

He huffs a laugh, pulling out and thrusting back in. "I get to own *you*." He wraps his hand around my neck, bringing his face close to mine. "I fuck the woman who gets fucked by no one."

"You don't own me." I tell him. "You just fuck me."

He laughs, thrusting again. "Whatever you have to tell yourself, kitten." He says, and then he fucks me into next week. He fucks me until the orgasm rips through me so hard that I'm begging him to stop, and still he keeps going, his fingers tightening on my throat with every thrust as he pounds into me before finally coming with a roar. My head thrashes from side to side, my pussy clenching with after shocks.

He pulls out, looking down at me as I lay sprawled on the bed. I'm a mess. He can ruin me in minutes, and while part of me fucking hates him, the other part is only too happy about the situation. His eyes flash behind the dark mask, dragging over my naked, sweat covered body. His chest rises and falls heavily, the dim light glinting off his dewy chest, his abs rippling with every breath. God, he's hot. He grabs my ankle, making me squeal as he drags me off the edge of the bed, just so he can slam his lips over mine.

"You're such a Neanderthal." I say when he's done.

He cocks a brow and turns away, showing me his broad shoulders and tapered hips. "Says the woman who likes to fuck a guy with a fake dick, for no other reason than feeling superior."

I sniff, shifting off the bed. "We all have our kink."

He chuckles as he pulls his boxers back on. They have showers here at the club and believe me, I feel soiled in the best kind of way, but I've never been able to bring myself to go in them. I mean, god knows what's been washed down the drains in there, even if it does look like a five star hotel. So I put my dress back on, the material clinging to my clammy body. He pulls his shirt over his broad shoulders, fastening the buttons quickly.

"See you next week stranger." I say with a teasing grin.

He grabs my arse, pulling me towards him roughly. I place my palms flat against his chest, feeling his hot skin. "I miss the way you fucking taste." He growls, making what might have been a romantic notion, and thus a crossing of the line, sound somehow dirty. He grabs my jaw, forcing his tongue inside my mouth until I nip at him.

"You've tasted plenty." I say, cocking my eyebrow and walking away from him. I click the door shut behind me and leave the club.

The problem with Landon is that I could easily get addicted, so consumed by him that it would be easy to lose sight of what this is, a temporary reprieve. Soon he'll go back to Dubai or New York or wherever the fuck else it is he lives, and I'll be here, in London, doing what I do best. I'm certainly not attached to him, but he brings something out in me that no one else does, an element of submission. When he pins me down and demands that I take everything he has to give, I like it. I always liked to dominate a man, but then maybe I've just never found a man capable of dominating me. I have to keep him on his toes though, just to remind him that I'm not the bitch that rolls over and plays dead.

THIS IS the pattern of our lives for the next few weeks. At work we're professional, above board, all good. I'm productive, I make money and for the most part I don't see much of Landon.

As soon as we step inside Masque, it's so easy, so simple, it's...freeing. There are no pretenses, no bullshit, just how I like it.

I sit in the boardroom with my laptop in front of me going over some spread sheets. I'm twenty minutes early for a meeting with Angus and Landon. Eva is supposed to be here taking notes again, but of course that girl always arrives at exactly the allocated time and not a minute before. I don't even look up when the door opens and then closes. I'm too busy focusing on the graph in front of me.

"Not even a good morning?" Landon's voice pulls my attention. He leans against the desk beside me and places a Starbucks cup in front of me. The rich aroma of coffee fills the room.

"Nope." I raise an eyebrow at him and pick up the coffee cup, taking a long sip. He chuckles, unbuttoning his jacket and slipping it off his shoulders before tossing it over the back of the chair next to me. When he turns his attention back to me I realise I'm staring at his chest. These are the times when our arrangement gets hard, when I'm alone in a room with him, and I'm picturing what that chest looks like without the material covering it, the solid muscles covered in smooth, tan skin.

"Georgia." I blink.

"Sorry, what?"

A wry smile makes it's way onto his lips and he pushes off the desk, circling around behind me and bending down until his breath moves the hair against my neck, tickling over my skin. "You have a terrible poker face, kitten." He says, his voice quiet but deep. "Keep looking at me like that and Angus is going to know."

"I'm pretty sure you're the one who'll get a bollocking where Angus is concerned." I say, glancing over my shoulder at him.

He stands and moves, taking the seat on the other side of me. "Ah, but I'm also the one who doesn't care who knows."

"Touche."

He leans over me and grabs my laptop, pulling it towards him. "Help yourself why don't you."

"I'm the boss." He grins.

"Yeah, you'd have thought you could afford your own laptop."

"Why bring mine when I can just steal yours?" His eyes flick up, meeting mine over the top of the screen, dancing with amusement.

"Why bring yours when taking mine is an excuse to aggravate the shit out of me, you mean?"

"So easy." He says, shaking his head on a smile.

"Arsehole."

"Temper." He quietly mocks, keeping his eyes on the screen.

The door opens and Angus walks in with Eva on his heels. Her eyes narrow darting between me and Landon. I haven't told her anything and believe me, sometimes I want to, but I don't know...I guess I'm almost ashamed of it. Quinn knowing is one thing because she doesn't know Landon, but Eva works here, she see's too much. She takes a seat at the head of the table on the other side of Landon and gets her laptop out, ready to take notes. Angus sits across from us.

"Okay, so this is just a catch up, nothing formal." Angus starts.

Landon slides my laptop back in front of me, revealing a solitaire game on the screen. Wow, really? I roll my eyes at him and he smirks to himself.

The meeting goes as they always do, standard shit. Landon does what he always does, which is flit between playing the boss and looking bored as shit. I can see now why he has so many businesses. He's great at what he does, but his attention wanes easily. I guess with a guy like him he has to mix it up to keep his focus.

When the meeting is done, Angus leaves and Eva lingers, waiting for me to take the lift back up with her.

"I need to talk to Georgia for a minute." Landon says as she hovers in the doorway. She glances at me briefly before she closes the door.

The second I'm alone with him, I become overly aware of him beside me. "What do you need?" I ask as I stand up, collecting my papers and laptop.

"Hmm, that's a loaded question."

I tilt my head to the side. "Really?" I sigh.

"It's Friday. You know what I need, kitten." Something

feral flashes in his eyes and it has my stomach clenching in the best way. Tuesdays and Fridays are when we meet at Masque, and the few days between often feel like torture. Like I said, I'm like a sick junkie.

"I know what you need." I whisper. He moves closer to me, stalking me, graceful yet deadly. He's close enough that I can feel the heat from his body caressing my skin like the softest of touches. My eyes drift to his full lips, surrounded by a five O' clock shadow that covers his chiseled jaw. I find myself leaning in, gravitating toward him like a magnet. Our lips are so close, and then I squeeze my eyes shut and press two fingers to his lips, breaking the invisible thread that exists between us. He releases a heavy breath and touches his forehead to mine for a second, and for that second, he doesn't feel like my boss, or even the guy I fuck, he feels like a possibility.

I pull away from him. "Tonight." I let my hand slip away from his lips, but he grabs my wrist, holding me in place. He turns my hand over, kissing the inside of my wrist. His lips are so gentle, sending tingles of sensation up my arm.

"Tonight." He says, and then he releases my arm, stepping back as though physically forcing himself to be out of reach. I leave with a nervous feeling in my stomach.

22

I don't bother going to Ice or meeting Quinn. I'm becoming increasingly more unsociable as the weeks pass. They say that a junkie can think of nothing but their next fix, well I think I'm there. Landon is slowly consuming my life and I'm willingly letting him.

I throw on a little black dress and a cropped leather jacket with a pair of Jimmy Choo ankle boots before leaving the apartment. I jump in my car and turn the engine on, putting it in reverse. When I put my foot down on the accelerator though, nothing happens. I frown and press it further and the car awkwardly limps backwards. What the hell? I chuck it in neutral and hop out only to find that my front tyre is flat. Well fuck.

Now, I'll be the first to admit that I have no idea how to change a tyre. It's just not a life skill that I cared to learn. I sigh and take my phone out, finding the number for the breakdown people. Well, it turns out that when you're on your own driveway they don't really regard you as much of an emergency, and it might take them up to two hours to rock up. I debate just calling a taxi and leaving it, but I'm going to need it over the weekend.

I pull my phone out and send Landon a text: *Don't know if I can make it tonight. Car issues.*

After a couple of minutes my phone rings, his name flashing on the screen.

"Hey." I say when I pick it up.

"Where are you?" His deep voice comes over the line.

"At my place, waiting for the guy to come and change my tyre."

He laughs. "You called someone to change your tyre?"

"Yes. I called someone to change my tyre. I'm not doing it."

He sighs heavily. "I'll be there in fifteen minutes."

"What? No..." The line goes dead and I find myself scowling at my phone. Arsehole. I go back inside because, really? What else am I going to do?

Sure enough, fifteen minutes later, the intercom buzzes.

I pick up the receiver. "Hello."

"It's me." Landon say, making me roll me eyes.

"You don't need to be here..." I start.

"Bring your keys down."

I hang up the receiver and pick up my car key from the side table by the door. When I get downstairs I spot him leaning against the side of a Maserati that's pulled up in the disabled bay. The midnight blue paint shimmers under the lighting outside the building. He stands casually, his legs braced apart and his hands propped behind him on the bonnet. He's wearing black jeans and a light grey shirt with the sleeves rolled up and the top two buttons undone. The whole thing looks like a magazine spread for Maserati.

"Nice car."

His lips kick up in a wry smile. "Thanks."

"You can go. I have someone coming." I say defensively.

"You do realize it takes ten minutes to change a tyre."

"Good to know."

He sighs and pushes away from the car, moving closer to me. "Okay, I want to fuck you tonight, no, I *need* to fuck you tonight." His eyes dance with something dark and feral. "So I'm going to change your tyre and then I'm going to take you to Masque and fuck you raw." I clench my thighs together as my underwear becomes soaked. Fucking shit.

I throw my car key at him and he lifts one hand, catching it without even moving. "The Mercedes." I say, pointing at my car two spaces over. He clicks the boot open, and moves away, standing by it as he starts unbuttoning his shirt. "Uh, what are you doing?" Jesus, what is he going to do? Fuck me right here in the car park? Images flash through my mind of Landon fucking me on the bonnet of that Maserati, and I have to bite my lip. Shit.

He shrugs the material off his shoulders. The dim street light plays over every chiseled line of his body. I can't help but stare. "Changing my shirt."

He pulls on a plain black t-shirt that's clinging to him in all the right places. Don't get me wrong, I like the suits but damn, he's making that look hot. He slams the boot and moves over to my car, opening the boot. "What are you doing now?"

"Changing your tyre." He says, ignoring me and proceeding to start tearing my car apart.

"By trashing my car?" He pulls back a compartment in the boot, revealing a tyre. So that's where it lives. He cocks an eyebrow at me, flashing me a smug look. "Fine." I sniff. He chuckles, shaking his head as he starts pulling various tools out of the boot.

I've never been much of a blue collar girl but I have to

admit, watching Landon throw around a tyre seems all very manly. When ninety percent of the men you meet have weekly manicures, it takes very little to impress me on the man scale.

He narrows his eyes and takes his phone out, shining the light around the hole in the boot where the tyre was sitting. "Where's the key for your locking wheel nut?" He asks.

When I don't respond he looks at me. "Are you seriously asking me that?"

He sighs and drags a hand though his hair. "Where did you buy your car from?"

"Mercedes. What key? This key?" I hold up the key in my hand and he actually rolls his eyes at me.

"No, it'll have to go to the garage and they'll have to saw it off."

"Saw what off?!" He ignores me and starts putting the stuff back in the boot.

"I'll get it sorted." He says dismissively. I fold my arms over my chest and scowl at him. He folds the floor of the boot back into place and shuts the boot. When he looks at me I'm still glaring. He smirks. "I could explain it to you, but you didn't even know you have a spare tyre."

"I did!"

He cocks an eyebrow at me, disbelief written all over his face. "Sure you did, kitten."

He braces his hands against the car and they're filthy from handling the tyre. There's a smudge of dirt on his cheek and without thinking about it I reach out and swipe my thumb over it trying to rub it away. The atmosphere suddenly changes, becoming instantly charged again. I should know better. I do know better, but sometimes with him what I should do and what I actually do don't seem to blend with no definition.

His eyes lock with mine and his fingers wrap around my wrist, pulling my hand from his cheek and pressing it against his chest, holding it there.

"You're covered in dirt." I say, my voice husky through my tightening throat.

He nods. "Can I use your bathroom?"

"Yeah." I hear myself saying. This is a bad idea. Landon should not be in my house. This is crossing one of the many lines that lead to my imminent failure at life, and yet I'm skipping the fuck over it.

He follows me inside and I notice him glancing around the apartment as I show him to the bathroom. I bought the apartment a couple of years ago when it was brand new. It's right on the river, very modern and as an investment, it's a smart one. But as I look around at it, seeing it through Landon's eyes, I guess it's pretty bare. To me, my home is a place where I sleep, but I've never been into trinkets. I keep my apartment clutter free and immaculate at all times.

I leave him to it in the bathroom and head into the kitchen. "Do you want anything to drink?" I shout, because it would be rude not to offer and he did try and change my tyre for me. Damn, I'm going soft.

"Do you have beer?"

"Wine." I offer. There's no response so I assume he didn't hear me. I take a bottle out of the fridge and pour a glass for myself anyway. When I turn around I plough straight into him. Damn it, I swear he's like some kind of ninja, always creeping up on me. I spend far too much time walking into his wall of a chest. He makes no effort to move and my pulse ratchets up about three gears.

"Wine's great." He says in that deep voice of his. I swallow heavily and turn around, squeezing my eyes shut as soon as I have my back to him. I pour him a glass and because he makes me jittery, some spills. He reaches around me, enclosing me against the kitchen cabinet as he picks up the glass. My skin prickles with awareness, and I have to force myself not to move. He moves away and I glance over my shoulder, watching as he takes a seat at the breakfast bar. He places the wine on the work top, pulls out his phone and starts tapping away on the screen before putting it to his ear.

"I have a job for you." He says into the receiver. "Yeah, tonight. New tyre and it needs to be back in the morning." There's a pause. "Put it on my account." He looks up at me, mouthing 'address'. I grab an unopened piece of junk mail out of the drawer and slide it across the breakfast bar to him. He reels it off and hangs up the phone. "He'll be here within an hour and tow it."

"Thanks. And you're not paying for it. Just get him to bill me." He says nothing and smirks as he takes a sip of his wine. "I mean it, Landon." I point at him.

"You know, if you want to do the whole independent woman thing, then learning how to change a tyre might be a good start."

I glare at him. "I am not changing a tyre."

He huffs a laugh. "What, too much of a princess?"

"I pay for breakdown cover for just such an occasion."

He shrugs. "Yep, and wait two hours for a guy to come and do a five-minute job."

"Well you didn't do it in five minutes."

"No, because you bought a car which is missing half of it's kit. I think they saw you coming, kitten." *Aggravating.* He's aggravating and irritating and annoyingly hot.

I choose to ignore him. "Well, thank you for your help. I think I can handle it from here."

He downs his wine and stands up, moving around the

counter and coming towards me. "I told you, I need to fuck you."

"Too bad. I'll have to reschedule." He moves even closer and lowers his face to mine. His scent assaults me, and his lips come so close I have to slam my eyes closed and grip the counter just to keep from leaning in and kissing him. "Unless you want to just skip the theatrics and fuck right here on the kitchen floor?" He breathes against my lips. I suck in a desperate breath as his lips brush over mine in a feather light touch.

I turn my head to the side. "What makes you think I would fuck you in my apartment?" A low chuckle makes it's way up his throat and he glides his nose over my cheek until his steady breaths touch my neck, making my skin flush with goose bumps.

"Very well." He sucks my earlobe into his mouth and nips it before pulling away. My lungs are screaming for air as I release a harsh breath and inhale deeply. I pick up my wine glass and down the entire thing. He laughs, his beautiful face becoming positively heart stopping beneath a wide grin.

"Do you have anything to eat?" He asks, opening my fridge, casually rummaging through it as if firstly; he hasn't just propositioned to fuck me on my kitchen floor, and secondly; it's his bloody house.

I slam the fridge door. "No, I don't. You need to leave." He ignores me and starts going through the cupboards until he finds some rice cakes and some peanut butter. "You know you're really annoying." I point out.

"And you're really uptight."

"I am not." He resumes his position at the breakfast bar and unscrews the peanut butter, breaking the rice cakes apart and dipping broken bits in the peanut butter. My OCD brain is having a melt down. I get a knife and plate and put them in front of him, sweeping up the crumbs and putting them in the bin. "Use a knife!" I snap.

He cocks a brow. "Case in point." He continues to dip the rice cake into the jar, a smug smile on his face the entire time.

"I swear to god, Landon…" I growl.

"Does it make you really mad, kitten?" He laughs. I storm towards him and make a grab for the jar but he pulls it out of reach.

"Damn it, will you just leave?" I shout.

"Just let it go." He purrs. *Fucking arsehole.* He dips a finger in the jar and then sticks it in his mouth, pulling it out slowly.

"You're disgusting." I grumble, making a dive for it again, this time he just holds it above his head and even with him sitting down I can't reach it. I stretch on tip toes and he laughs the entire time as I lean over him. Suddenly his free arm is in the small of my back and he pulls me until I topple forward against him with my hands braced on his shoulders and every inch of my body plastered to his side.

My anger subsides and his grin disappears as his eyes drop to my lips. I hear the jar clink against the worktop and then his hand is in my hair and his lips are a whisper from mine. I feel like a yoyo with him, backwards and forwards, wanting him, then hating him and back again.

"Let go, Georgia."

I squeeze my eyes shut but don't pull away from him. "I can't."

"Then let me make you." I don't even have time to register his words before he grabs me around the waist and picks me up, dropping me on the edge of the breakfast bar and stepping between my legs.

"I can't…" He drops to a crouch in front of me and forces my legs open at the same time, popping the stitching on my skirt as he presses his lips against the lace over my clit. I choke, unable to talk, or think. All I can do is feel him, his fingers digging into my thighs, his warm breath on my skin, the promise of his lips, his tongue. His fingers slip beneath the lace, sliding over my pussy.

"Landon. I…" Oh god, he makes everything feel so good. "Not here." I say, though the words are lost on a moan as he pushes two fingers inside me.

"I can stop, kitten. Just say the word."

"I can't fuck you here." I plead.

He thrusts the fingers harder into me and I buck wildly. "You're not fucking me Georgia. I'm just having a taste." And then his face presses between my thighs as he yanks my underwear to the side and swipes his tongue over my clit. I tense even as a wave of pleasure rips over my nerve endings.

"Let go." He murmurs against me. I have no willpower left, and how could I against him? Landon plays me like an instrument, his mouth and fingers working me over like a master. I don't stand a chance. He breaks me, changing me into a person I don't even recognize.

His tongue circles my clit as his fingers thrust into me. My pussy is clenching around him and a low growl tears up his throat. He has me falling apart in minutes, my arms braced behind me and my back arching off the work surface. My fingers are pulling at handfuls of his hair as I come, every muscle shaking and clenching. When I'm done he bites the inside of my thigh hard enough to leave a mark and pulls his fingers out of me. I'm panting and shaking as I lay there staring at the spot lights above me.

I refuse to look at him but I can feel his eyes on me. I'm

about to say something when his phone rings, breaking the silence.

"It's the guy for the car." He says. I simply nod before I hear his heavy footfalls as he moves down the hallway. He starts talking to the guy on the phone and I hear the clink of my car key before the front door slamming.

Oh my god. What am I doing?

Landon doesn't come back. Instead I get a text from him about half an hour later: *Kitten. It was getting late so I left. Your car is taken care of. Meet me tomorrow night? I can still taste you and I need more.*

I *always* need more. That's the problem.

It's Saturday morning, and I think I'm having a small mental breakdown about last night. What is it about that man that makes me flick the middle finger at everything I've always known? My rules, my job, my life...he makes me forget about it all, as if everything I ever wanted suddenly doesn't matter. Then he leaves and I'm left wondering what the hell I was thinking. The problem is, I don't think around him. He tells me to let go, but he doesn't realize that the second I met him was the second I lost my grasp on every single thing.

I go through my usual routine: make coffee, get dressed, pick up the post...only this time there's an envelope in my mail box, and it has something heavy in it. I open it to find a note and a key fob with a little silver trident on it.

Georgia,

My guy can fix your car without sawing the nut off, but you can't have it until Monday. Use mine until then. I'll see you tonight.

L x

I glance out the window and sure enough, parked in my space is the midnight blue Maserati. I squeeze my eyes shut and inhale through my nose. And now this. As if everything else wasn't enough, now he does things like this, and I think it's worse, because this is an act of kindness. Last night he was selfless. I need to hate him, but it's becoming increasingly harder.

23

By the time I finally walk into room 12 in Masque, I'm horny and irritable, but mostly confused. Landon came into my house, I let him into my house. Then he went down on me, made me come and left without so much as a goodbye. Why does it bother me? Because men are sexual creatures, driven by the simple urge to empty their balls into someone. What he did, it goes against the entire nature of our agreement. Perhaps if his phone hadn't rung he would have tried to fuck me. Maybe I would have let him. Right there. In my apartment.

He's standing by the bed, removing his cufflinks when I walk in. He looks so calm, so controlled, the same as always. I don't want control. I want him to feel as unhinged as I do.

I close the distance between us and slam my lips over his so hard that he staggers back a step. I push him and he falls back on the bed with a low grunt. His eyes burn into me from behind the mask and for the first time since we started this, I feel powerful. I lean over him, dragging my nails over his hard stomach before I yank his belt open roughly. He cocks a brow, watching me with a hint of amusement in his expression. I pull his trousers and boxers down just enough for his cock to spring free. Before he can move or say anything I kneel between his knees and slide the thick erection between my lips. A strangled groan makes its way up his throat and his hips buck as his dick touches the very back of my throat. I swallow around him to keep from gagging and suck my cheeks in as I slide back up. His fingers dive into my hair and he lets out a string of expletives. I don't suck cock very often, but trust me, I'm very good at it. For the first time since I met Landon Banks, I'm in control. I own him right now. With an act that I have always seen as submissive, I'm now dominant.

I swirl my tongue around the tip and he jerks violently beneath me. "Fuck, Georgia." He hisses. I work him over until he's a mess, groaning and writhing beneath me. I want to make him come. I want him to lose all sense of self until the only thing that exists is me, my mouth, my touch. But just when I'm sure I have him, he sits up and grabs my hair, yanking me away from him. I look up and our eyes lock, wild lust sparking through his like an angry storm cloud, rolling and swirling dangerously.

"I want to come in your pussy, kitten." He pants.

I push to my feet and reach behind me, unzipping my dress and pushing it off my shoulders, allowing it to pool at my feet. I remove my bra and thong until I'm completely naked, standing in just my heels. His eyes survey every inch of my body hungrily as I throw one leg over his thighs, straddling him. The hot skin of his torso presses against me and tingles of sensation skitter over my body. Leaning forward he presses his lips against mine, but I pull back and fist his hair allowing him only a feather light brush of his lips over mine.

"Don't tease." He growls, and I smile, because I've never

seen him so on edge. I lean in and suck his bottom lip into my mouth, biting down on it as I lift up on my knees and fist his cock. He hisses out a breath against my lips and I smile, releasing his lip. He allows me to pull his head back further and swipe my tongue up the side of his throat as I lower myself down on his cock. My head falls back as a breathless gasp slips past my lips. Oh god, he feels so good. Every time. It doesn't matter how many times I fuck him, it feels like the first time, every time, as though my mind is being blown and my body is being torn apart and put back together.

"Fuck!" He shouts when I take all of him. I release my grip on his hair and trail my hand over his jaw, cupping his face. His eyes meet mine and something passes between us, a connection unlike anything I've ever felt. And if I'm honest it scares me, so I start to move, clinging to his shoulders as I ride him. I moan as I grind my hips over him in deep, slow strokes. Hot breath mists my skin as his lips skate over my chest. His strong arms wrap around me, his forearms braced between my shoulder blades as his fingers knot in my hair. He pulls me close until there's not an inch of space between us. I press my forehead to his, closing my eyes. His lips find mine, swallowing the string of moans that leave my lips as he forces his cock deeper inside me. My pussy clenches around him and my core tightens as pleasure tears through my body, making me come so hard that I see stars. His hands slip to my hips, pushing me over him harder and faster as I scream. A feral growl works its way up his throat before he stiffens, thrusting deep inside me one last time and collapsing back on the bed. My head falls forward and I brace my hands on his chest, absorbing the after shocks that are rippling through my body in waves.

"I need to see you more." He says out of the blue.

I open my eyes and look down at him, frowning. He

remains impassive, his gaze focused on the ceiling. "You see me most days."

His gaze meets mine. "I'm not talking about the office. Twice a week isn't enough, kitten." How much is enough with an arrangement like this?

"You could always go and fuck someone else between our meetings." I say, though the words bother me when I know they have no right to.

He sits up, bringing us face to face. I grip his shoulders and he starts twirling a strand of my hair around his finger absentmindedly. "Is that what you want?"

I shrug and focus my eyes over his shoulder. "I fuck Apollo." I say, completely avoiding the question all together. I fuck Apollo with Landon watching, as a way to try and hold onto the control that Landon strips me of. He's a walking catch twenty-two. I like what he does to me, but then hate that I allow it.

His lips twitch. "Hmm, but you're hot when you play at having a dick."

"This isn't suppsed to be a habit." I say quietly, unable to look at him. I would happily fuck Landon every night of the week, but where is the line? A night here and there quickly escalates into every other night, and then what? It's not good for either of us, but I'm the one with everything to lose here. He risks nothing.

"Well then I propose a new contract." He says. Just like that.

He reaches up and gently trails his fingers across my cheek as he tucks my hair behind my ear. It makes me frown and a whisper of concern takes hold. Things are changing.

He tilts his head to the side, meeting my gaze. "What's wrong?"

I shake my head. "Uh, I...I need to go." I swing my leg

over him and sit on the edge of the bed, searching for my underwear. He inhales loudly, shifting on the bed and moving behind me. His fingers wind around my throat from behind, and he drags my back up against his chest.

"Landon..."

"Did I say I was done?" He growls right against my ear, snapping from the guy I could like into the arsehole I want and loathe at the same time. A shiver creeps over my skin and my pussy clenches.

"*I'm* done." I hiss back.

He huffs a laugh. "Wrong, kitten. You're so fucking wrong."

And he proves me wrong, because we're so far from done. Landon and I may never be done. But this I can cope with, this side of him, I like, because I can still hate him. The guy that holds me while I come and tells me he needs to see me more...the guy that lends me his car and goes down on me, wanting nothing but to make me come...that guy I can't handle, because that's a guy I could like. That guy has the potential to damage me.

24

QUINN and I usually do the gym or yoga in the mornings, every other Monday though, we do coffee. The Monday that I'm with Giles, she tends to schedule a Tinder date. She tells me it's the only way to date in the city, but honestly, the thought of meeting complete randoms, most of which just want to send dick pics and spank one out to the thought of your tits...yeah, no thanks. She assures me you just have to dig through the shit ones to find the occasional gem, but that sounds like far too much effort to me. Not to mention the fact that she clearly hasn't found a keeper yet. This coming from the girl who fucks her boss though...I'm in no position to judge.

"Have you seen this?" Quinn drops the *Daily Mail* on the table in front of me and takes a seat.

I frown and glance over the pages, my eyes going straight to the image of Landon with a dark haired woman, his arm wrapped around her waist and her head resting on his shoulder. The picture is grainy as though it was captured from a distance. I skim over the article, not wanting to jump to conclusions, but if anything, the fact is worse than the fiction I had concocted in my head.

"He's married?!" I ask, ice leaking into my voice.

She shrugs one shoulder. "They say all the good ones are already taken. Hot, loaded, *and* good in bed. If you think about it, it would actually be freaky as fuck if he were single."

"Wow." I don't really know what else to say. He's married and he didn't tell me, but then why should he? We're just fucking, and even that is with a big dose of plausible deniability. His apparently broken marriage is none of my concern, and yet...it is. It shouldn't bother me, but it does. Shit.

"She's some catwalk model or something. I heard he cheated on her and now she's trying to take him for all he's worth." Upstanding guy.

"Well, if they're too stupid to spot a player when they see one then what do they expect." I say, swallowing around the lump in my throat, because for all the times I've said that, mocked and chastised other women for being so blind to their perverted husbands and partners, that woman has never been me. I have never been made to feel like the other woman. I'm not now, so why do I suddenly feel used? Jesus, if anything it's me using him. At least that's what I try to tell myself.

"Are you okay?" She asks, her eyebrows pinching together in a frown.

I nod once. "I'm fine. I have to go."

I stand up and bend over, kissing her cheek quickly before I leave. I know she knows I'm not okay, but because Quinn is a good friend, she says nothing and lets me go.

I get in my car and drive towards the office, but I'm ridiculously early, not to mention totally confused, so I stop at Berkeley Gardens, a few streets away from the office and spend half an hour walking around the Gardens. I try to clear my head. I really do, but the more I think the more I find myself making assumptions and decisions which I really can't do when I only have half the information. Or perhaps that's just me hoping that there is an explanation of some sort, because I don't want to be that person that got fucked over.

When I get to work I make-up a hundred excuses as to why I don't need to be in my office. I pick up a pile of documents that are packaged in envelopes and go down to the mail room in the basement, which is ridiculous because not even the assistants go to the mail room, the interns do it. Once I'm done getting funny looks off the guy who works there I go down the street and pick up coffee for me and Eva, and then...nothing. Turns out there's really not a lot for me to do outside of the office. I sigh as I walk slowly back to Mayfair house, clutching the two cardboard cups in my hands.

When I take the lift back up to my office, I swear I can feel my heartbeat increasing with the rising floor numbers on the little screen. I keep my head down as I cross the office, ignoring everyone. Great, my paranoia over Landon is now spreading to every-fucking-body in the building.

I put the coffee down on Eva's desk. She glances at it before following the length of my arm, and looking up at me. "I was wondering where you were." She stands and follows me into my office, pushing the door closed behind her.

I drop into my chair and pull up a proposal I was working on yesterday.

She drops an envelope on the desk in front of me and it makes a heavy thud. "Some guy dropped this off for you."

She says. I open it and find my car key inside with a note telling me that my car is parked in Mr. Bank's parking space. He has his own space? I shove the note and my key in the top drawer.

"So..." Eva starts, letting the word linger in the air.

My eyes flick to her, watching as her eyebrows hike up. "So what?"

She moves around the desk and sits on the edge of it facing me. "Landon. Wife." She takes a sip of her coffee, swinging her legs back and forth like a child.

I move my gaze back to the computer screen and stare at it, seeing nothing. "Yep. I heard."

"And you're not bothered?"

My gaze snaps back to her, my eyes narrowing. "Why would I be bothered?"

"Please," She snorts. "I know you have a thing for him, possibly with him. I haven't worked it out yet." I release the breath I was holding.

"He's my boss." I say flatly. "I have no *thing*."

She tosses her long red hair over her shoulder and shrugs. "You still look at him like you want to fuck him." Her eyes flick over my face. "Don't be embarrassed. Hell, we all look at him like that. But with you, he gives it right back." Her lips pull into a small smirk as she cocks an eyebrow.

I turn back to the screen, twisting my entire body so as to put my back to her. "I need the print outs for last week's figures on the McGuire account." I say, dismissing her.

She lets out that tinkling laugh of hers. In my periphery I see her hop of the desk with a little bounce. "Sure thing boss." She says, amusement lacing her voice.

"Oh, and can you have this sent up to Susan?" I take the Maserati key out of my handbag and hand it to her. She eyes the key with an incredulous look on her face, but doesn't say a word. She's learning.

I work through the rest of the day, but I'm on edge, and I don't really know why. Come five thirty I decide I've had enough. I normally don't leave until after seven but ever since Landon came charging into my life, I've found myself skipping out way more than I should. Of course I'm contracted until five, but you don't get anything in this life unless you work for it and seeing as I want the fucking world, the long hours are necessary.

I'm just dropping my phone and iPad into my handbag when there's a knock on the door.

"Come in!" I shout. I'm expecting Eva to walk in, the same as she does every day just before she leaves, but when I look up it's not Eva.

Landon lingers in the doorway looking unsure of himself for the first time since I met him. "Are you okay?" I ask.

He frowns and closes the door behind him before walking over to me and stepping very close, too close. I immediately step back and tilt my head to the side, flashing him a questioning look.

"I'm sorry." He says. He looks...angry, but he also looks as though he's fighting it.

"For what?" I ask.

He drags a hand though his hair and blows out a breath. "You know what. My wife." That word, wife, suddenly sounds offensively loud.

Hearing the words from his mouth makes them somehow seem worse, but really this is a good thing. I don't even know what we are anymore, the lines have blurred so far that they're nothing but a smudge on the ground. Seeing that article made me realize that somewhere along the way I stopped hating Landon. It's myself that I hate. I feel oddly connected to him, addicted and we both know that our interactions in that club have gone beyond sex. He wouldn't be here apologizing otherwise. We're carrying on this strange relationship behind the closed door of room number 12, and if the rest of the world didn't exist, then it would be perfect. But it does exist, and he has a wife in it. This is the point where I should tell him I'm out, I'm done. God knows I've said it enough times before, but a stubborn corner of my mind refuses to. To leave now would be to acknowledge that this is more than what it should be. Leaving now would imply that him having a wife is an issue when it's not, or at least it shouldn't be. So I slide on the mask that I've worn for years, slipping easily into the façade.

"I don't care." I say.

"You don't?" He asks.

I lift my gaze to his on a sigh. "You're my boss. What you do is your business." I move to step around him but he moves into my path. His gaze locks with mine and his usually calm demeanor seems to bristle, the power he wears like a perfectly tailored jacket shifting and morphing into something more. I want to flinch away from him, but I force myself to stand my ground. His hand moves, cupping the nape of my neck and forcing me to look at him.

"I'm not here as your boss, Georgia." He says, his voice rough. It takes me a second to remember where we are, to react. I stagger back a step.

"Then we have nothing to discuss."

His jaw tenses and he drops his gaze to the floor. "Fuck!" He shouts, making me jump. He pinches the bridge of his nose and paces in front of the desk. "Just for a second, be fucking straight with me, no bullshit, no role play, no boss and employee, no *masks*. Just you and me, Georgia and

Landon." I say nothing, because this is dangerous territory. The rules, the lines, the contract, they're what makes this work, and right now, he's threatening it. His eyes meet mine and there's a slight vulnerability in his eyes. "We're separated and have been for over a year." He says.

I steel myself and look up at his face. He looks troubled and I can see the anger flashing behind his irises. "Landon, you're my boss." He opens his mouth to object. "And a couple of nights a week, inside a sex club, hidden behind a mask, I'm the woman you fuck." I stare at him. "Nothing. More."

He watches me silently, and I wait. I know I'm cold, but I have to be. His wife is none of my concern and the fact that he thinks she is, is cause enough for me to be worried. I shouldn't be the woman whose feelings he's concerned for.

"I hope you manage to sort it out." I say, and then I force myself to turn around and walk away, for both our sakes.

25

LANDON and I don't speak for several days, and that's not uncommon during the work week, but I always see him on a Tuesday. On Tuesday afternoon he texts me and tells me he can't make it. No explanation. I come to find out from Angus that he's in Dubai for a couple of days dealing with divorce solicitors. He never misses our meetings. I know I have no right to be pissed, but I am. I keep thinking about him with his wife and each time, a stab of jealousy hits me. Of course then I feel ridiculous for thinking that, and so it goes, round and round in a vicious circle. I ignore his text and carry on with my life, because it doesn't revolve around bloody Landon Banks.

Finally on Thursday there's a knock on my office door. I don't even get a chance to answer before he strides right in.

"Landon." I say quietly. He always looks gorgeous, but today...damn. Maybe it's because I haven't seen him in days. He's wearing a steel grey suit with a black shirt underneath and a matching grey tie, all perfectly pressed, not a crease to be seen. His hair is just a tiny bit too long, the dark waves falling messily over his forehead. I glance at his face, those sharp cheekbones seeming to pop out as he purses his full lips. I think my ovary actually just twitched. No man should have the right to look that good. Especially not when I'm mad at him for so many reasons.

He approaches my desk and slides a pocket folder in front of me, bracing his arms on the edge of desk.

"What's this?" I ask.

"The itinerary for our trip." His face remains completely impassive.

"What trip?" I open the folder and read over the print, a schedule that starts tomorrow morning with a flight from Heathrow to New York. "You want me to go to New York?"

He nods. "I need you to help me secure Montgomery Lavare." He wants me to go to New York with him. No word from him for days. He's the one with the fucking wife, and yet somehow *I* did something wrong. *Arsehole.* And just to make matters worse, I'm horny as fuck, and now he's going to be out of the country for our usual Friday night meeting. Or maybe he planned this. Maybe he thinks he can drag me into some trip and turn a business trip into a dirty weekend. Well, he can go fuck himself.

I take a few deep breaths—in through the mouth, out through the nose. I have to remind myself that this is work, and that if I can't separate my personal feelings, mainly rage, towards him and my professional feelings, then I shouldn't be doing what I'm doing.

I squeeze my eyes shut and focus. Montgomery Lavare. He's a billionaire who owns half of London and is making his way through New York. I'm pretty sure that in my extensive stalking (research) on Landon I saw somewhere that they went to school together.

"You don't need me to close that. I don't know the guy." I argue.

He drops into the seat across my desk and clasps his hands behind his head, leaning back casually. "He likes pretty things. It will help."

Oh, he did not. I feel my temper bubbling just below the surface. I know he's trying to push my buttons, so I turn away from him, focusing on the spreadsheet on the computer screen.

"I'm busy this weekend. I need more notice than..." I check my watch. "Eighteen hours." I click print on the computer and stand up, moving to the corner of the office where the printer sits. The machine noisily works away and he remains silent until it's finished.

"If we close this, it will exponentially increase your bonus." He says right behind me.

I spin around to face him, a glare fixed on my face. "I don't need your money, Landon." I snap.

"You're a stock broker." His eyes burn into mine. The longer he stares at me the tighter my chest becomes.

"Exactly. Not a cheap whore who you can ask to flash a bit of cleavage in the hope of signing a client." I try to shove past him, but he moves with me, blocking me with his body.

"Is that what you think I'm doing?" He asks, his voice calm.

I turn my face away from him, focusing on the door, anything that isn't him. I flinch when his hand brushes over my cheek, his touch making my skin flush with goose bumps. He brings my face back to his until we're only inches apart. "Is that what you think?" He repeats, his breath touching my lips. I swallow hard, my eyes dropping to his mouth.

"I don't know what to think." I step back awkwardly. His hand falls from my face and once again we find ourselves in grey territory, dancing along the line and just waiting to fall over it.

"Lavare likes strong women. That's all." He says, ducking down in an attempt to make me look at him.

"I don't want to go." Shit, I can't go. In the office with people watching it's easy for me to remember that he's my boss, but even then I slip up. It's easy to remember all the reasons to keep it in my pants and wait until we're at Masque, but in New York half the world away with no one watching...I don't trust myself in the slightest. I might as well just fuck him right here on the desk and get it over with.

He sighs and drags both hands through his hair. I skirt around him, making my way back to my desk. I feel safer around him if I'm behind my desk. I need something between me and him. "Don't make me pull rank, Georgia."

My temper spikes and I bite. "Why the fuck do you want me to go?" I growl. "Take Leanne with you."

He narrows his eyes. "Why are you so set against going?" He asks. "And I don't want Leanne. I need you."

I brace my arms on the edge of the desk and drop my head forward, allowing my hair to fall over my face like a curtain. "That's what I'm worried about." I mumble before lifting my head. "Fine. I'll come, but I want a good cut on bonus, you will pay for me to have a separate room, and you will remember at all times the stipulations of our contract." I scowl, pointing my finger at him.

A wicked smile pulls at his lips. "Of course." He looks like the devil himself, so sinfully sexy and ready to lure me off the path of my thriving career. I'm fucked.

The next morning I step out of my building at six thirty and hand my luggage to the driver standing next to the black town car at the curb. Landon is on the phone when I slide into the back seat, his headphones in as he types away on his laptop, reeling off figures to whoever is on the other end. He carries on his conversation whilst picking up a cup of coffee that's wedged into the cup holder between us and handing it to me without even looking at me. I take the cup, cradling the warm cardboard in my hands as the aroma of strong coffee beans hits me. *Thank god.* Okay, so right now I like him, sort of. It's more of a mild tolerance.

"Please tell me you're joking." Landon suddenly growls into the microphone on his headphones. There's a pause as whoever is on the line responds. "You tell him that if that share value drops by more than two percent I'm going to bury his company." His voice is eerily calm and I think it's more scary than when he's being all growly. He yanks his earphones out and slams the laptop shut, releasing a heavy breath.

"Thanks for the coffee." I say, holding up the cup. He glances at me and nods. "You know it's way too early for that shit." I gesture to his laptop.

"New Zealand." He says as way of explanation, dragging his hand over his face. Of course, they're fourteen hours ahead of us I think.

We don't really talk on our way to the airport and that's fine with me. I have no desire whatsoever to talk to anyone at this hour. The car rolls to a stop outside the terminal doors, and I hop out, waiting for the driver to haul my suitcase out of the boot. Landon cocks a brow as he looks at the case.

"You do realize we're away for two days?"

I roll my eyes. "You're a guy, you wear the same thing for every occasion."

He pops the handle up on my suitcase, slinging his weekend bag over his shoulder.

"Take this." He says, thrusting his laptop bag at me before he walks off, wheeling my suitcase behind him.

"You know I can take my own suitcase." I say, trotting after him, struggling to keep up in my heels.

He keeps walking, refusing to look at me. "It's too early for your independent woman bullshit, kitten."

My mouth falls open and my step falters before I jog to catch up with him. "You did not." I hiss.

"I did." He says, still ignoring me. Oh my god. I'm going to stab him before this trip is over. I can feel it.

Eight hours later and we touch down in New York. A town car picks us up and takes us to the hotel right in the middle of the city, over looking Times Square. Some people might think it's a good view, but it's more like having a fucking disco in your room while you're trying to sleep. I've been to New York City far too many times to appreciate the light show.

True to his word, Landon has booked us separate rooms, although there is an adjoining door in the middle. I want to say something about that, but he did bring my suitcase all the way up here, so...

He checks his watch. "We have dinner with Lavare in an hour. I'll come and get you." And then he leaves. God, this is weird. I've never had to spend any time with Landon that didn't involve either a business meeting, or him naked and me with my legs spread. The plane ride was awkward for the first hour, so I just got to work, organizing some figures that I've been meaning to do for a few days.

I open my suitcase, pulling out the dress bag and hanging it on the wardrobe door before I start stripping out of the soft cotton dress I travelled in. I leave a trail of clothes as I make my way to the bathroom. There's a massive bath tub that I can't resist, so I switch on the taps, pouring some sweet smelling bubble bath in the water. I step into the water, resting my head on my knees as I wait for the tub to fill. The scalding water rises, easing the stiffness in my muscles from sitting still on a plane for seven hours.

Half an hour later and I feel ready to face the shit show of me and Landon.

I dry and straighten my shoulder length hair and slip into the blood red dress that I brought specifically with this dinner in mind. Clients like Lavare are predictable, born of old money. They can't just cut the shit and do business, oh no. They like to fanny around with niceties, a dinner the day before you have a business meeting, because heaven forbid you should just get down to it. It's the tactful side of the business that I've never been very good at.

I swipe some matching lipstick over my lips and check my reflection in the mirror one last time before I slip my heels on. Landon knocks on the door a few minutes later, and I grab my clutch bag before I swing the door open. His eyes pop wide as they drag over my body.

"You look...good." He says, his eyebrows pulling together in a deep frown. I roll my eyes and push him out of the way, so I can close the door before making my way down the hallway.

We step inside the lift. I make every effort to ignore him when he moves close to my side. Inside Masque, he's like my own personal salvation. He's a breath of fresh air, something freeing and thrilling that I crave wholeheartedly, but outside of those four walls he's a thorn in my side, a constant reminder that I'm not as strong as I think I am. After the whole wife debacle I'm really starting to resent him, whilst hating myself for even caring enough to feel slighted. Big. Fucking. Thorn.

We take the car a few blocks over to a restaurant. I forget how long it takes to get anywhere in this city. You either sit in bumper to bumper traffic or you walk. And I don't do walking because I don't own a pair of flats.

The restaurant is one of those places that you probably have to wait for months to even get into. Landon gives Lavare's name to the hostess and we're shown to a table in the back. Lavare stands when we approach. "Landon, it's been a long time my friend." He says, the slightest hint of a French accent entwining with a heavier American accent.

"Lavare, this is Georgia Roberts, she's the best broker I have besides Angus, but you know he doesn't like to leave the island." He says jokingly.

I know Lavare is the same age as Landon, late thirties, but Landon looks late twenties at a push. Lavare has whispers of grey appearing at his temples and fine lines marring his forehead. He's a small man, and almost elegant in the way he presents himself. He takes my hand, touching his lips to the back of it. I try to keep the smile on my face, but it's hard, it really is, until I notice the way that Landon's lips have pressed into a firm line.

"Lovely to meet you." I say with far too much sugar in my voice. God, I'm almost making myself feel sick.

We eat, we drink wine, we talk. I spend the entire time ignoring Landon and charming the pants off Lavare, exactly like he wanted me to. The more I talk to Lavare, the more flirtatious it becomes and the more Landon's mood seems to decline.

After we've eaten the waitress approaches the table with

a dessert menu in hand. "Would you like to see our dessert selection?" She asks with a polite smile.

"No." Landon snaps. "Thank you. We uh, we should get going." He offers Lavare as way of explanation. They pay the bill, shake hands, whatever. Lavare again kisses my hand, his lips lingering just a little longer this time.

"I so look forward to working with you, Miss Roberts."

"Likewise." And then it's done, and we're leaving the restaurant. Landon says nothing as we walk to the car and the silence continues the entire way back to the hotel. I can feel the tension and anger radiating off him like a beacon, and if anything the silence is only making it worse, but I refuse to acknowledge him. He wanted me to come on this trip. He told me to work Lavare and that's what I just did. Maybe next time he'll think twice before using me.

As soon as the car pulls up at the curb I throw the door open and get out, walking straight through the hotel lobby to the lift. I wait impatiently for it to arrive, tapping my toe against the marble floor as I do. Long seconds pass and still it doesn't arrive.

"Damn it!" I growl, slamming my hand over the button again even though I know it won't help.

I turn around, pacing one way and then the other until Landon steps in front of me, forcing me to come face to face with his broad chest. "Will you stop?"

I take a deep breath, inhaling the smell of his after shave like some creeper, and then I force myself to step back. I'm mad at him. He's mad at me. It's all a cluster fuck and the last thing I need is to be lusting after him. The lift pings and the doors slide open. I step inside and he follows.

Two businessy looking guys are already inside and their eyes blatantly skate over my body, their tongues practically rolling out of their heads. One of them actually makes it to my face, where I make eye contact, staring him down with my best resting bitch face. A red flush creeps from under the collar of his shirt, making its way up his face until he's scarlet. A satisfied smile fights its way onto my lips before I turn around, facing the doors. Landon leans against the side of the lift, a scowl permanently fixed on his face. He glares at the two guys, but apparently not satisfied with looking at them like a murderer, he grabs my arm and pulls me into his side. I don't fight him because it's fucking embarrassing, so instead I slip my hand inside his jacket and find his nipple, pinching it and twisting through his shirt. He flinches away from me, but he's backed up against the wall with nowhere to go. He glares down at me, an uncomfortable look crossing his features. Good, I hope it fucking hurts. I glare right back at him.

The lift doors open a few floors up and the two guys get out. The second the doors close he turns, pinning me up against the wall he was just standing against.

"Don't..." I kick out at him, catching him in the shin. "Fucking touch me." I huff, shoving him away from me.

"A nipple cripple, really?" He asks, his face thunderous.

"You touched me!"

"Because that guy was practically fucking you with his eyes." He snaps.

"So? I'd rather that than you touch me."

"Really, kitten? Because I've touched you plenty." He mocks.

"Gah! That doesn't count here!" I scream.

"Do you have some sort of mental deficiency?" He asks.

"Go fuck yourself, Landon."

The lift doors open and I storm out, walking as fast as

my heels can carry me. He easily catches up to me just as I slide the key card into my room door. I shove it open and go to slam it in his face but he's already barging through right behind me.

"Get out!" I shout at him.

He sighs and crosses his arms over his chest. "What is wrong with you?"

"Nothing is wrong with me. You just..."

"I what?" His expression is serious, completely focused on me.

"Please just go." I beg, refusing to look at him anymore.

"No. You're pissed. You've been pissed since Monday, even though you lied to my face and told me you were fine. So you tell me now what's wrong, and I'm not leaving this room until you do." I can't tell him what's wrong. I can't tell him that it bothers me that he has a wife, that I'm annoyed that he failed to mention that, and yet I have no right to be mad about it. I can't say that I'm pissed off that I haven't seen or barely heard from him all week. I can't tell him that I'm annoyed that he wasn't there on Tuesday to fuck me. I can't voice any of it, so I say nothing.

"You don't know me, Landon. Don't suppose to."

He huffs a laugh and drags his hand over his stubble covered chin. "I don't need to. An idiot could see your mood from a mile away."

I clench my fists. "Are we in Masque right now?" I snap. His eyes tighten in response, but he doesn't answer the obvious. "No, we're not. Which means right here, right now, you are my boss. We are not friends. You don't get to judge my mood, and you don't get to be pissed about the fact that I was overly nice to a client that you purposefully used me to bait!" By the time I'm done I'm shaking a little, my blood pressure spiking.

His turbulent eyes meet mine and I can see the storm lingering just below the surface. "He was looking at you like he wanted to eat you." He grates, his jaw tense. "You draw all these fucking lines, kitten and you expect me to just fall within them."

"Yes." I say coldly. "I fucking do." He turns away from me and makes me jump when he slams his hand against the door violently. "Those were the terms of the contract you laid out." I say to his back in a desperate bid to stop whatever this is right now. But it feels so inevitable, like a runaway train hurtling along the tracks at full speed. Men like him, they set the stipulations, they don't follow them.

He spins around, storming me until I'm pressed back against the window with his hand around my throat. His lips are so close to mine, his angry breaths blowing raggedly over my face. He's this close to snapping. I can feel it and I can see him fighting it. "Fuck the contract." He spits. The words feel like a gunshot on a silent night, ripping through the air, leaving only the echo of my silent scream in its wake. The train officially just went careening off the tracks and exploded in a ball of fire. "For one night just fuck it." His voice drops almost to a whisper. Something deep down inside me, buried in a place I didn't even know existed surfaces, a sense of want, wanting of something foreign and unknown. I slam the lid on it, closing it down as quickly as it started. And then I'm angry. I'm angry at him for even suggesting it. I'm angry at him for putting me in this position, for upturning my perfectly mapped out life, and most of all I'm angry at myself for being so damn weak when it comes to him.

Instead of screaming though I feign a laugh. "Oh wow. What did you think would happen here, Landon? That you'd get me to New York and have me on my back in a hotel room for the entire weekend? Your dirty little bit on the side." I hiss, pushing against the restraining hand on my throat until my lips brush against his. "Did you think I'd get on my knees and give you everything your wife won't?" I lower my voice to a husky whisper.

He slams me back against the glass so roughly that my head ricochet's off the window. "So that's what has you so riled." A satisfied smirk pulls at his lips and I want to slap him and then slap myself for letting him get to me.

"I'm not your office whore, Landon, so I'm afraid I won't be spreading my legs for you tonight." I say, desperate to dig the knife in somewhere anywhere, because he always seems to have the upper hand.

He brings his face close to mine, his gaze fixing on me. "I don't need to fuck you, Georgia. I just don't want you to look at me like I'm a fucking business transaction." There's just a hint of vulnerability in the way he says it, as vulnerable as a guy like Landon can be, and it pulls me up short. I want to feel indignant, but I can't.

"How else am I supposed to look at you?" His eyes lock with mine and his grip on my throat slowly loosens.

"Just because you want clear lines doesn't mean you have to hate me." God, but I do, because it's not hating him that led me here, giving a shit, feeling hurt and down right bloody pathetic.

"I think I do." I admit, lowering my gaze. His hand moves from my throat to the back of my neck, his fingertips trailing over my skin.

"Stop overthinking it." He says, his lips brushing over mine. "I like you, Georgia. I respect you, and yes, I want to fuck you, but I thought we were friends if nothing else."

I close my eyes and my lips part, my body gravitating

towards him. I drop my head forward and he pulls me close, pressing his lips against my forehead. I clench my balled up fist against his chest.

"We're not friends, Landon." I whisper. "I know nothing about you. You know nothing about me. I didn't even know you were married, and you know why? Because I'm the whore you fuck. Nothing more."

He pushes a finger under my chin and forces me to look up at him. His expression is soft, his eyes full of concern. "You have no idea how fucking wrong you are."

"Am I?" I ask, because if he really stops and thinks about it, he'll see I'm right.

"Okay. Fine. Lets just...hang out." I pull back and frown at him. "As friends." He clarifies. "No sex, no work, just this." He gestures between us, and I frown. "Not everything has to be black and white." And he's right. A part of me secretly wants to know something more about Landon. Maybe I just don't want to be his whore, or maybe I just hate the idea that he has a wife who knows everything about him while I know nothing. So I slowly nod and he releases his grip on me, taking a concerted step back with a small smile on his face.

"What do you want to do?" He asks, backing up and taking a seat on the bed. "Do you want something to eat?" He asks.

"Uh, we just ate."

He scoffs. "That was enough food to feed a three-year old. How is it that the more money you pay for your food the less you get?" And just like that, we fall into an easy dynamic. I let my guard down. I let myself appreciate Landon's company and that's something I've never allowed myself to really do, not properly.

In every game there is a game changer, a pivotal point that turns the tide of the game. I think this is it. This is the point where this could go two ways, but neither of them are a desirable outcome and I don't want to face that possibility, so I choose to ignore it. For right now. And I'll deal with the rest when I get home.

Landon orders a ton of food and puts a film on.

"So, you said I know nothing about you. Tell me." He says, scoping a piece of cheesecake into his mouth. I'm sitting at the top of the bed and Landon is lounging on the sofa, with the food.

I shrug. "There's not a lot to tell. I grew up in London, went to University there and have spent every moment since working to get where I am."

"Family? Friends?" He leans back into the sofa cushions, unbuttoning the top two buttons of his shirt. My eyes dip to the little V of skin at his chest.

"Quinn is my best friend. My parents are dead." I don't elaborate. It's not like I was ever close to them. I spent my childhood being raised by Au Pair's. My mum got cancer when I was eighteen and my dad died of a heart attack two years later. I hate talking about myself because it makes me realize how pitiful my life really sounds. Landon pointed it out to me the first time we really spoke...it's lonely at the top, but these are the sacrifices I have willingly made.

"What about you?" I ask, trying to deflect his attention from me.

He puts his empty plate down on the coffee table and gets up, sitting at the end of the bed and laying down. "My dad's kicking around somewhere, we talk sometimes but he's..." His lips pull into a cooked grin. "He's busy getting married and divorced. He's on wife number six."

"Wow."

He laughs. "Yeah. Stand up guy. My mum died a few years back. I have a brother who is the polar opposite of me and is currently helping children in Africa or some shit."

"And a wife." I add.

He sighs, dragging a hand over his face as he fixes his gaze on the ceiling. "Yeah. I was like you; focused, determined...obsessed. I had no one and I needed no one and I was happy with that. When I met her though, she made me feel like maybe I did need *someone*. She was strong, beautiful, had a solid modelling career, and I respected her, which is rare."

"This is sounding familiar." I mumble, pulling my knees up to my chest and leaning back against the headboard.

His lips twitch and he turns his face towards me. He's lead on his back, sprawled across the bottom of the bed. The TV is on playing quietly in the background but neither of us is watching it. "Turns out I didn't want her, and I certainly didn't need her. It all went to shit within a year really, but I was away working all the time. I barely saw her, so we ticked along for three years. I prioritized my businesses over her, because that was and is my first love. I never loved her, I just married her because I thought I should."

"Mid life crisis?" I smirk.

"Something like that. Anyway, I served her papers last year and she's been out for blood ever since. Apparently she deserves half of every business I own." He sighs. "Word of advice, don't get married."

I say nothing, and instead focus on the duvet beneath me, tracing circles on the material with my nail. Long moments of silence pass.

"Say something, Georgia."

I shrug. "I don't know what you want me to say." I pull

my knees up to my chest and lean back against the head-board. "It is what it is."

"I want you to say that you understand, that you're okay with it."

"Why wouldn't I be okay with it?"

He huffs a laugh and drags both hands through his hair, focusing his gaze on the ceiling. "Because you're human." I frown and he looks at me. "And if your little outburst earlier is anything to go by, you're not okay with it."

I shake my head. "I just hate being played, and I won't be used."

He sits up, leaning on his elbow. "Is that what you think?"

I sigh and drop my head back against the heavy wood of the head board. "We use each other Landon."

His eyes study mine before he finally nods. "Okay, but I'd still be annoyed if I found out you had a husband."

"So, what? Now you want me to be pissed off about it?" Jesus, what is with him?

He curls his hand into a fist and drops his gaze to the bed. "I...I don't know."

Well fuck, I'd say we left black and white half the world away in London, because right now we're swimming in an ocean of grey.

Neither of us says anymore about it, but we don't need to. Once said, words can't be taken back. We've already said too much.

We watch a film and I fall asleep right there with him in the bed. When I wake up, his arm is wrapped around my waist, pinning my body against his. He stayed true to his word. He didn't try to fuck me or even get me naked. I'm still wearing the shorts and tank top I changed into before he put the film on. He nuzzles into the back of my neck and I clutch the arm that's around my waist, holding him to me. I want just one more minute, one more minute to pretend that we're just two people with no lines. The worst thing is that him holding me like this feels so right. It's the hardest thing in the world, to experience a taste of what you know you can never have, what you can't allow yourself to have.

26

"Tell me, Miss Roberts, why should I trust you with my money?"

I slow smile creeps over my lips as I stare Lavare down. "Because I'm the best." He leans back in his seat, steepling his fingers together as he watches me. Landon remains silent at my side. "And I happen to know that you're down five percent on your rather sizeable investment in The Renworth Corporation." His brows pull into a frown. "Not to mention the eight percent you lost when you bailed on Atlantic Energy."

"How do you..."

"I know the market, Mr. Lavare. I know where money will make more money, and both of those companies were a sinking ship long before you put your hard earned dollars into them. A good broker should have seen that." I love this, the thrill of the chase, it's what people like me live for.

I slide the folder across the desk to him. "There's my proposal, Mr. Lavare. Read it over and contact us." I stand up and he watches me like he just found something fascinating. I walk out of the room and wait outside as Landon wraps up.

I'm leaning against the wall in the corridor when he closes the door and approaches me. "You never fail to surprise me." He says.

I feel awkward around him. I'll openly admit that I am totally out of my depth and I don't like it. For the first time in my life I feel vulnerable. He's punched a hole in my carefully constructed wall and we're looking at each other through it, him waiting on the other side for me to come out, and me hoping that he'll go away. But he's not going away, he's standing his ground in true Landon style. So for now we're at this strange impasse, a sort of limbo if you like.

"Damn, Georgia, crack a smile would you? You just landed Lavare."

"I did?"

He cocks a brow. "He's sending over the paperwork this afternoon.

"Good. That's...that's good."

He grins and shakes his head as he makes his way down the corridor. I follow him, staring at his arse like a raging pervert the entire time.

He presses the button and we wait. He seems completely at ease, while I feel anything but. "What now?" I ask.

He checks his watch. "Well the flight isn't until this evening. We should do something."

I frown. "Like what?"

He chuckles as the lifts doors slide open and he steps inside. He turns around and looks at me. "It's New York, kitten. The options are endless."

I scowl at Landon as we pull up on fifth avenue. "Really?"

He laughs. "Told you you're uptight."

"A sex museum?"

He continues to laugh as he throws the car door open and gets out. I'm not getting out. He opens my door and folds his forearms over the door, standing on the other side of it and peering in at me.

"Oh, come on, kitten. It's just a few pre-historic dildos."

"Oh my god, Landon."

He laughs, throwing his head back. "Come on." He grins. He seems so at ease that I actually feel bad saying no. For fuck's sake.

"Fine." I huff, climbing out of the car. He offers me his hand but I ignore it.

He follows me to the curb where I stand looking up at the building. "I want to make a deal." He says behind me.

I turn to face him. "Oh? What kind of deal?"

He drags a hand through that sex idol hair of his. "I want you to stop." I frown. "Just stop thinking."

"Uh, can you be more specific?"

He smirks. "Everything with you is like a fucking quadratic equation. But life isn't an equation, kitten. Sometimes you have to just go with it."

I don't really know what he's asking me. "It's not an equation Landon, it's simple, you're my—"

"Not today." He shakes his head. "I don't want to be your boss, Georgia. You have no idea how much I wish I wasn't. But right here, right now, let's just be us. Fuck the labels."

"Fuck the contract." I whisper.

A slow smile pulls at his lips. "Fuck the rules."

He's so bad for me. So dangerously bad.

He wraps an arm around my waist and leads me to the

door of the museum. The first thing we see when we step inside is a statue of two pandas fucking.

"Wow. You brought me to see some kind of panda porn."

He laughs. "It's art."

"No, this is fucked up." He ignores me and goes to the ticket desk. He can pay for this, because I sure as hell am not parting with any money over this shit.

It gets worse though. There are contraptions and as he predicted, pre-historic dildos. I stop at a monstrous wooden one.

"I'm envisioning splinters." I say.

He snorts. "That thing has to be fifteen inches long and it's the splinters your worried about?"

"Good point."

We move on until we're standing next to some kind of sex chair set up in the middle of the room.

"Don't even say or suggest anything." I warn. He chuckles and wraps his arm firmly around my waist again. Every time he does that I tense and I'm sure he notices, but he doesn't acknowledge it.

He leads me through the 'museum' and we see more freaky shit, bondage equipment, paintings of penises, a sort of motorized dildo which looks like it would hurt a lot, and finally antelopes having a threesome. Yep.

He moves behind me, placing his hands on my hips and pulling me back into him as if we're a normal couple at a normal museum, looking at an exhibit. Except we're not. We're us and we're looking at a statue of an antelope three-some. This pretty much sums us up.

"I just want you to know that if this is your idea of a date then no wonder you're single."

His lips brush over my neck and my skin prickles as

goose bumps rise on my neck. "I didn't think you were the dating kind."

My breath hitches and my heart rate picks up. I shouldn't let him this close, but I can't pull away. He gently kisses my neck and my eyes shutter closed as a low hum of electricity buzzes over every nerve ending. "I'm not." I breathe. I'm not, but for him I could be...if I let myself.

"Neither am I, but never say never. Certain people have a way of changing your mind." It's right there all hanging in the air between us, spoken in half riddles and assumptions. I turn to face him and his eyes meet mine, burning into me. "You could change my mind." And there it is, his cards, laying on the table in front of us. I want to throw mine right down next to his, but doing so would ruin everything, so I hold onto my denial. I keep my cards close to my chest and I say nothing.

"Landon, I..."

"Stop thinking." He whispers. His hand cups my cheek, his thumb rubbing over my jaw as his eyes drop to my lips. I don't want to think. Right here, right now we're in our own little bubble, away from London, away from everything, and I want to pretend that this is something real and tangible. So I lean in and press my lips against his. A low groan makes its way up his throat as his hand moves to the back of my neck, pulling me closer. I stop thinking, and I just feel. I feel everything that lies between us, the longing, the lust, and more. As I kiss Landon in front of the antelope three way I realize that I think I've fallen in love with him. Shit.

Neither of us has spoken since we left New York. In the moment, while we were there it was like living in a dream, one where the possibilities are endless and anything goes. But now we're back in London, and reality is crashing in like an unwelcome yet familiar friend. I find myself wishing we could erase the last two days from both our memories, but words are like the pulling of a trigger, once said they can never be taken back, never be unheard, and the damage they inflict may be beyond repair.

We're picked up at the airport by his town car. Again we say nothing as the car moves through the London streets. It's four o' clock. The city at this time of morning is eerily quiet. The car eventually rolls to a stop outside my Greenwich apartment, the engine idling as the driver waits patiently.

The long moment of silence has me fidgeting nervously. I don't know what to say to him any more. This can't keep going the way it is. I hate to admit it, but there are feelings involved here, anger, jealousy, longing, lust...*love*. They're all right there staring us in the face, and yet neither of us want to acknowledge it openly because we both know that the second we do this is done. It has to be. I'm about to tell him I'll see him at the office on Monday when he speaks.

"Come to the club tomorrow night." He says it more as an order than a question.

"I..." *Tell him no. Tell him no!* I glance at him and my heart beats just a little harder. I don't want to say no, even though I know I should. Fuck, of all of the people in this city of eight and a half million people, it just had to be him, the one guy who should be unequivocally off limits.

"I'll text you." I breathe, and then I'm getting out of the car. The driver gets my suitcase and the car remains at the curb until I close the front door to the building.

I turn my phone off for the rest of the weekend.

27

IT's Monday morning so I'm meeting Giles for breakfast. He's already here when I walk into our usual coffee shop. I make my way over to the table in the window. Giles likes to people watch, he calls it a hobby. Yeah, he's strange. He's already ordered me a coffee and he pushes it in front of me when I take a seat at the table.

"You look tired, Georgia." He comments without even looking up from his paper.

"I'm fine. Jet lagged."

He closes the paper and folds it, smoothing his hand over the face of the publication. "You should take a vacation. You know I have a house in Bali. You could even take my private jet."

I smile. "Well, thank you, but appealing as that sounds I can't go."

He shrugs, lifting his coffee to his lips. "The offer is always there. You could even take that young man." He lifts his eyebrows and sips his coffee conspiratorially.

"There is no man." I roll my eyes.

"Really?" He pops the paper in front of me and opens it

to the gossip section, stabbing his finger into the page. Fuck, really? There's a picture of Landon and me walking out of the restaurant where we met Lavare for dinner. Of course, the tabloids are all over this at the moment because his ex-wife is not only a model as Landon said, but she's Isla Marie, otherwise known as Isla Banks, world famous catwalk model. As if it wasn't bad enough.

The article simply refers to me as a mystery woman. *Great.*

"That was a business meeting." I say defensively. "He's my boss."

He chuckles and folds the paper again. "A man can be your boss and still bang you." His accent makes the words sound comical.

"No. No banging." I say with a smirk. He's a nosy old git but luckily for him I love him. "How's your wife?"

"Well, talking of banging..."

Oh, gross.

28

I DON'T HAVE to wait long for the shit to hit the fan. I leave Giles, spend a few hours at work and go to La Carte with Eva for a working lunch. I'm scrolling through emails and Eva is jotting down a list of things that need immediate attention when a woman moves into my peripheral vision and stops at our table. I stop what I'm doing and glance at her. She's tall and thin, wearing skin tight jeans and strappy heels. Her long dark hair falls around her face in perfectly orchestrated waves as her dark eyes fix on me. She's beautiful, and I've seen enough in the media to know that she's Landon's wife.

"Can I help you?" I ask, trying not to sound like a raging bitch, but my hackles are up. There is no possible good reason for her being here.

She smirks, crossing her arms over her chest. "So you're the whore that he's fucking at the office."

"Whoa." Eva says.

I stand up so that I'm more of a level with her but damn, the bitch is like a fucking giraffe. "Isla Banks, I presume?"

"Yes. I am." She holds up her left hand showcasing a monster rock and a wedding band.

"Well, word of advice, don't make an arse of yourself until you know the story. He's my boss. We're friends." I don't know if she can see the lie written all over my face or not, but her jaw clenches and her cheeks flush pink.

She gets in my face, eyeing me up and down. "I'm going to take him to the cleaners for this. He'll lose everything, all for some little *whore*." She hisses the word with so much venom, but beneath the mega bitch front, I can see that she's hurt, more than that, she destroyed. Men like Landon will do that to you. I glance nervously around the restaurant, worried that she's drawing attention. A few people glance in our direction but luckily it's not busy in here.

"Look, you need to talk to Landon. This is none of my business."

"No, it's not. So kindly close your legs. He might fuck you, but he'll get bored. Sluts like you are ten a penny. Disposable." I lose my shit. This is one of those moments where you should be the bigger person, where you should stop and think, but I don't. I lash out. One minute she's standing there and the next my hand has connected with her face and her nose is pouring blood as she's screaming bloody murder.

"Oh, shit!" Eva says behind me. I stand there in shock for a moment before she drags me away, out of the restaurant with Isla screaming at someone to call the police because she's been assaulted. When we're on the street Eva starts laughing. "Holy shit, G."

"Oh my god." What did I do?! I'm finished. She'll press charges and then I'm fucked.

I pace backwards and forwards in my office while Eva sits on my desk, watching me.

"You're fucking him aren't you?" She asks.

"That's really not the fucking issue right now!" I say, spotting a smudge of red on my dove grey dress. I want to cry. How has this all fallen to such shit in such a short space of time?

"Look, he'll help you. You have to go to him."

"And say what?" I throw my hands up. "That I punched his wife? Fuck!"

She shakes her head. "She deserved it, but I'd bet she's pressing charges as we speak."

"Look, just give me a moment, please." I drag a hand through my hair and sit at my desk. Eva hops off it and makes her way to the door, flashing me a concerned look before she pulls the door shut behind her.

I pick up the phone and dial Quinn's number. I never thought I would need a solicitor, but now that I do, having a friend who is one is helpful. She picks up on the third ring.

"Quinn." I say her name, my voice breaking.

"George, what's wrong?" I don't know whether it's hearing her voice or just everything, but a single tear slips free, tracking down my face.

"I fucked up." I choke, before explaining the situation to her.

She listens without interrupting, and of course up until the point where I hit her she pretty much knows the story. "I need to leave." I say, because I desperately do.

"No, look, if she presses charges then at least wait and see what she wants. She probably doesn't want you away from her husband. The marriage is already over. She wants to point the finger so the court will rule in her favour, and you just helped with that. She'll play the victimised wife and milk it for all it's worth."

I shake my head. "You didn't see the look on her face, that is not a woman just trying to get money. She still loves him."

She sighs. "Look, you need to speak to him. This could play out so many different ways, but either way, you're a means to an end, George."

"Okay. Thanks. I'll call you later."

I fire off a text to Landon: *I need to speak to you. Now.*

He texts back straight away: *Angus is out for the afternoon. Come up to the office.*

By the time I push open the door to Landon's office I know exactly what I'm going to do and I'm shaking because I'm about to lose everything. Even now though, he makes everything seem...inconsequential and irrelevant.

He pushes up from his desk and strides across the room, moving with that savage grace of his. His jacket is slung across the back of his chair and his shirt is clinging to his narrow hips, the sleeves rolled up exposing the muscles that rope his forearms. His eyebrows are pulled together in a deep frown as he approaches. He opens his mouth to speak, but I cut him off.

"I hit her." I blurt. "Your wife approached me and I hit her."

His eyes go wide before a slow smile makes its way onto his face. "Seriously?"

I slap his chest, and when he starts laughing I slap him again. He grabs my wrists, pinning them together against his chest with one hand. "Fuck you, Landon." I say, my voice trembling.

His expression becomes serious and he ducks down, trying to force me to look at him. When I don't he grasps my chin and tips my head back, forcing me to meet his gaze. "Don't go falling apart on me, kitten."

"I can't do this anymore." I whisper. And I can't. I've tried to keep things simple but they've become more and more complicated. I don't like complicated. I don't like this knotted feeling in my stomach that replicates the tangled threads of my life all jumbled together in one fucked up mess. I just need to be free of it all. I'm going to walk away, and that's so much harder than it should be. I'm here to tell him that. I just need a minute, just one more minute of him.

He releases my wrists and wraps his arm around my waist, pulling me against him. I bury my face in his chest and inhale the smell that is all him. It comforts me when I know it shouldn't, but fuck it, what does it matter now? I fought so damn hard against him, and yet I'm still going to lose it all. And not because of him, because of me.

"It'll be fine. I'll fix it."

"No. She said she's going to take you to the cleaners." I mumble into his solid chest.

"So you hit her." His chest vibrates under my cheek.

"No. She called me a whore, and then I hit her." He cups my cheek, pulling my face out of his chest and focusing his gaze on mine. His dark eyes dance with amusement. When he looks at me like this I feel invincible, like nothing can touch me, all because Landon Banks wants me.

He strokes his thumb over my jaw as he cups my cheek, and then he leans in, pressing his lips to mine in a whisper of a kiss. He kisses me as though I'm everything to him. He kisses me like he would move mountains and conquer countries for me. It might all be a lie, a beautiful lie, but I want to believe it. I want to let my cold heart feel just a flicker of warmth for a fleeting moment. His thumb strokes rhythmically over my jaw as his lips linger over mine. When he starts to pull away I grasp handfuls of his shirt, pulling myself closer to him and slamming my lips to his so hard that our teeth clash. He strokes the hair off my face, his touch gentle but firm as his tongue traces over my bottom lip. I want what he gives me, that sense of security. I want him to make me feel as though the world starts and ends with us, one last time.

Before I can overthink it, I start unbuttoning his shirt, my fingers working easily down his body, parting the material as I go. I don't know what I'm doing, I just know that I need this. My palms press against his bare stomach, the skin like fire beneath my touch. He groans against my lips when I rake my nails over him. His hand slides to my back, lowering the zip on my dress. The kiss becomes more frenzied with my desperation. He tears his lips from mine and grabs a handful of my hair, wrenching my head to the side. I gasp when his lips hit my neck, sucking, licking, kissing as I try desperately to drag a full breath into my lungs. His fingers work beneath the material at my shoulders, shoving the straps of my dress down my arms until it pools at my waist.

I push his shirt off his shoulders and drag my hands over the thick muscles of his chest. Everything about him makes me want to fuck him. Just the sight of him has my stomach clenching, my heart hammering and my lungs feeling as though they're paralyzed. And when he touches me like this, the world falls away, everything focusing on the point where his skin meets mine. Nothing else exists.

He wrenches my tight skirt up over my thighs and then steps back, pulling the entire thing over my head. He pauses for a second, taking in my black lace lingerie and thigh high stockings. A devilish smile pulls at his lips as he shrugs out of his shirt and steps up to me, his bare torso pressing against mine and sending sparks of electricity rippling over my skin. His fingers brush over the strip of lace that surrounds my thigh at the top of my stockings, a low growl slipping past his lips.

"Fuck, I want you like this all the time." He groans, before his fingers grip my thighs roughly, lifting me until my legs are either side of his waist, my lace covered pussy pressed against his lower abs as the heat from his body makes me wet and needy. He moves, and there's the clattering sound of objects hitting the ground as he swipes everything off his desk including the computer. My back hits the desk, and his body is arching over me as I wrap my legs around him, pinning him to me.

"I've pictured you on this fucking desk so many times." He breathes against my skin, working his lips over my jaw. This is the one place I swore I'd never be, on his desk like a slutty secretary. But what does it matter now? This, us, our secrets and lies, it's all done. I just want him, not the guy in the mask—him. Just this once.

I fist his hair with one hand, bringing his face back to mine and thrusting my tongue inside his mouth as I work my hands between us and unfasten his belt.

His trousers are pushed down and then his hand is diving beneath the slip of material covering my pussy, yanking and tearing it away. My heartbeat is sky rocketing and my skin is over-heating with each passing minute.

And then there's a pause. He touches his forehead to mine as one strong hand grips my hip, the other cupping my cheek. I've been fucked every possible way by Landon, but this is different, this is something else entirely. Our breaths intermingle, our hearts beating in sync as he slowly slides inside me. I clutch the back of his neck, holding him close.

This right here is what I've been running from so hard,

so why does it feel so right? Why now, of all times, does he have to feel so vital to me?

He moves inside me slowly, his strokes long and deep. I feel like I'm sinking into him, falling into an oblivion where everything is perfect and safe and nothing else matters. He kisses me while he fucks me, dragging everything out of me that I have to give, and when I come, I cling to him as though he's a raft in a stormy sea, because truthfully he is right now.

He stiffens above me, groaning my name against my lips as he comes. I lay there with my eyes closed and his dick inside me, and I know that the second I open them this is over. This was goodbye. Truthfully it tears at something inside me, something that I didn't even know existed.

"Kitten." He presses a kiss on my forehead before he pulls away leaving me empty and alone. I tear my eyes open and sit up. Without looking at him I walk across the room and scoop up my dress, sliding it over my head.

My hands are shaking as I try to fasten the zip. My eyes are prickling as tears threaten to form. *I will not fucking cry!* Landon has shattered me and put me back together again, and the worst thing is, he'll never even know. He'll never know how much he meant or how he made me feel. He'll never know how close he came, how close *we* came. But sometimes you have to know when to walk away.

I like Landon. Hell in a different world I might love him, maybe I do love him in as much of a capacity as I have, but whatever this is I feel for him, its has too many complications. The bottom line is: I now face being unemployable because I hit his wife. I never thought I would be that girl. There are a lot of things I never would have done before him, but here we are.

His hand brushes over mine, pushing it away from the zip and easily zipping the dress.

"Thank you." I whisper, afraid that if I speak now my voice will crack.

"I'll fix this, Georgia. I promise. Isla won't be able to touch you by the time my attorney is done with her."

I turn to face him, plastering a smile I don't feel on my face. "Okay." I feel like a shitty person right now, pretending it's all fine when in reality I've already given up.

His brows pull together in a frown as his eyes lock with mine. "Please just trust me."

I wish I could, I really do. "I have to go."

His hand wraps around my neck, his lips brushing over mine gently. When he breaks the kiss, I turn and I walk out of that room as fast as my legs will carry me. It's only once I'm inside my office do I allow the tears that I've been fighting so hard to fall. I only have myself to blame.

29

THAT NIGHT I pack up my desk into a little cardboard box and take one last glance around the room. I take a piece of paper and fold it in two staring at the blank white space, the pen in my hand hovering over the paper. What do I even say to him? I think I'm in love with you but your wife is a bitch, so bye? Shit, this shouldn't be this hard. I bite my lip as tears sting my eyes. You can spend your whole life obsessing over the details, planning everything to the letter, but nothing could have prepared me for him. For this. I always knew this would end badly, but I never imagined that walking away from him would feel like I was slamming a knife into my own chest. I press the pen to the paper and write the only thing I can possibly say, because anything else is nothing more than a pathetic excuse, and he knows better.

Landon,

I'm sorry.

G x

I pop it on the desk, pick up my box and leave. I don't look at anyone as I leave and I don't stop until I'm at my car.

In the next few hours I email an immediate resignation

to Angus, simply telling him to ask Landon why. That might seem like I'm being a bitch, but I'm not. Landon can tell him whatever he wants, but it's his choice how much he wants to tell. After all, he's the one who still has to work with Angus. Personally I think Angus deserves the truth. Then I change my phone number and my email, letting Quinn and Eva know the new ones. It might seem extreme but I need a completely clean break from him. But I know him, he'll want an explanation. I could be wrong. For all I know he just moved onto the next, but I don't think so.

The next morning my door bell rings and when I open the door, there on the doormat is a manila envelope. When I open it, I find that I just got served by Isla Banks' attorney.

Life changes in the blink of an eye, and the best you can do is dust yourself off and get the fuck up. I can't apply for any jobs until I resolve this shit with Isla. The last thing I want is to get a job and then a couple of months in, I've suddenly been slapped with an actual bodily harm charge. Because that looks so professional.

Quinn has been over here going through things with me. We made Isla an offer of twenty grand to settle outside of court, she turned it down and made it very clear she doesn't want to settle. So I don't think there's any way out of it, but Quinn seems to think it will be a slap on the wrist. Probably an anti social behaviour order and court fees. That doesn't help me though, I wouldn't hire someone with an ASBO.

It's now Thursday evening and we're drinking wine and watching re-runs of Game of Thrones because the girl has a serious obsession.

"Are you okay, George?" She asks out of the blue.

I smirk. "As okay as you can be when your life is ruined."

"Have you heard from Landon?" The sound of his name causes an ache in my chest, like an old injury flaring up after you think it's healed. I've blocked him out, all thought of him, all trace of him. I'm good at denial.

"No. Why would I?" I say, focusing my gaze firmly on the TV screen.

"I just wondered whether there's anything he can do."

I shake my head. "I don't want his help. I'm the one who hit her and I'm the one who will deal with the consequences."

"But..."

I turn my head and lock my eyes with hers. "I don't need him, Quinn." I snap. "Landon is not an option anymore." I rub at the spot over my chest where it feels like a blade is wedged between my ribs. Every time I her his name it's like someone is twisting it. She watches me for long seconds before she nods slowly. She's as bad as Eva, who insists on calling and telling me everything that Landon does. He's asking about me, he's left the country, he's pushing through the divorce. I don't need to hear it.

It has taken everything for me to stay away from him. I spend hours sometimes staring at his number on my phone, fighting with myself not to call him. Realistically though what would I even say? My life is spiralling out of control. I feel broken, and I so desperately crave his implacable strength, for him to put me back together and hold my shattered pieces in place. But that's exactly why I won't go to him. You can only ever rely on yourself in this life. I did before him and I will now.

30

It's late on Saturday night when there's a knock on my door. I put my laptop down on the coffee table, getting up to answer it.

Eva and Quinn are on my doorstep wearing dresses and heels, *short* dresses and *high* heels. "Uh, hey. Did we have plans?"

"Nope." Eva pushes past me, in a scrap of red material so small I'm pretty sure it's actually a top. She waltzes into my living room and glances at my laptop screen. "Oh my god, G. It's a Saturday night and you're doing work for clients that are still with a company that you don't even work for anymore..."

Even Quinn cocks a judgmental eyebrow at me. "I'm just helping Angus. I left with no notice." I defend.

Eva rolls her eyes. "Whatever. Go. Wash. Get dressed. We're going out."

"Why?" I ask.

They glance at each other. "We thought you might need cheering up with your job and the case and everything." Quinn says.

"You need to get back in the saddle. Best way to get over one man is to get under another one." Eva pipes up.

"No." I shake my head.

"Yes." Eva grabs my shoulders, spinning me in the direction of my room.

"Really? This is so unnecessary." I argue as she forcibly pushes me into the bedroom. "Can't we just stay here?" She grabs the hem of my shirt and starts lifting it, but I snatch the material away from her.

"Don't make me undress you!" She points at me, raising her eyebrows. Jesus, she's scary sometimes. She's like an evil, angry little ginger.

"Fine!" I grumble as she leaves the room.

"And shave your snatch!" She shouts from the living room.

Oh my god.

———

Eva drags us to some dive bar that she knows. The music is loud, the floors are questionably sticky and the drinks are bright colours, but no one knows me, and that's good.

"You girls need to learn how to let loose." Eva says as she approaches our table, placing three tequila shots down before going back to the bar and bringing me a martini. She places a Cosmo in front of Quinn and has some bright blue concoction with an umbrella in it for herself.

"Bottoms up." She says, lifting a tequila shot. Quinn and I glance at each other, picking up the shot glasses. We all clink glasses and then I'm pouring what tastes like paint stripper down my throat. Oh god.

Two tequilas and two martinis later and I've decided that getting drunk is a great way to get over my entire fuckery of a life. I mean, why not? It's not like my reputation isn't fucked anyway. A fist to the boss' wife's face will do that for you.

"So...." Eva starts. "You fell for the big boss, then hit his wife and now you're jobless and soon to be in possession of an ASBO?" She asks, sipping on a bright blue cocktail. I shrug and nod, necking half of my third martini.

"And now you're becoming an alcoholic." Quinn slurs. "And apparently like any good captain I'm going down with the ship." She giggles.

"How am I the ship?"

She shrugs one shoulder as she takes a sip of her Mojito, shivering and glaring at the drink as she puts it back down. "This tastes like shit."

I pick up my martini and neck it, before signaling the bartender for another.

"Shit." She groans, gulping back the cosmo and making a face.

"You guys wanted me to get shit faced." I point at the two of them. "So I'm dragging you down to my level."

She flashes me an exasperated look before getting up and walking to the bar.

Two hours later I'm clinging to Eva's arm and attempting to look sober as we approach the door for Q.

"Stop stumbling." She hisses.

"I'm trying." The bouncer eyes us up and down, probably because we're dressed like hookers. I have on skin tight black leather trousers that I bought ages ago but haven't been brave enough to wear, and my stomach is exposed by the tiny white lace top. I don't even care. I'm drunk.

I flash the guy a smile and he waves us on through dismissively.

"Lets dance!" Quinn shouts from the other side of Eva, throwing her hands in the air.

She forces her way through the crowded dance floor, stumbling against people as she does.

Q is in what used to be one of the council buildings before they moved to one of the sky scrapers. The dance floor sits beneath a massive domed ceiling, surrounded by a circle of marble pillars. The VIP section is an over hanging second level that runs around the outside of the building. There's actually a lift that comes straight up from The Mayfair Club into the VIP, but The Mayfair club is not a place you go when you're in the state I am.

Quinn pulls me with her and starts grinding against me, her hips moving in time with the music. Eva ducks out, heading to the bar for another drink.

A few minutes later and a guy moves in behind Quinn, gripping her hips as he dances with her. His eyes flick over my shoulder just as another pair of hands touch my waist, because of course, men come in pairs. I'm drunk, so I'm okay with it. I dance, I laugh, I press my back against the guy. I don't know what he looks like, and I don't care right now, he's just someone to dance with. His hands move down until he's griping my hips and pulling me back against him. Warm breath blows over the sweat slick skin at my neck, making me shiver, and for a moment, my drunken mind pretends its Landon. I lean into him more, bowing my back and pressing my arse against him. His hand moves up my front, brushing over my boob, but it's not possessive, it's tentative. It's not Landon, and it never will be.

I turn around, ready to tell him to fuck off, but I don't have a chance. His lips slam over mine and my reflexes are too slow to see it coming. One hand goes to the back of my neck, holding me in place even as I try and push away from him. He tries to force his tongue in my mouth but I clamp my jaw shut as I continue to shove at his chest. Then suddenly he pulls away, no, he's dragged away.

I narrow my eyes as I watch the scene in front of me. The guy is standing facing me, a few feet away, but his angry gaze is focused on the figure standing in front of him with his back to me. All I can see of the newcomer is dark hair and a very well tailored shirt. The tension between the two is palpable, and I'm pretty sure a punch is about to be thrown. A few words are exchanged and the guy goes to step forward, but stops when a large hand is placed on his chest. He glances at me one last time and then leaves. I wait, standing still amongst a sea of dancing people. My rescuer glances over his shoulder at me, and, of course, its Landon. My heartbeat picks up at the sight of him and that stabbing pain rips through my chest. His eyes trail over my body once before his expression sets into the cold, steely mask that has never been reserved for me...until now. An uncomfortable feeling settles in my gut, a fissure of panic wrapping around my chest, constricting me. I suddenly feel very sober. I take a step towards him, more out of instinct than anything else, and then he turns and walks away, becoming swallowed up by the crowd. I search for him, but he's gone and all I'm left with is the haunting memory of the look on his face. Disgust. Regret.

I walk out of the club without a word to Eva or Quinn and get straight in a taxi. I need to go home. I need to fix my life, not get wasted drunk and start grinding over random strangers. It just reminds me that no one will ever be him. It reminds me of how far I've fallen and how much I've lost, because Georgia Roberts wouldn't do that. I don't even know who I am anymore, and Landon just looked at me like he doesn't either.

31

I'm MEETING Giles this morning for our usual Monday morning breakfast.

I take a seat and order a coffee.

"I hear you're in a spot of trouble." He says, as serious as I've ever seen him.

I sigh. "Says who?"

"Landon called me." *Great, just fucking great.* No doubt he's told him that this ship is sinking fast and he needs to jump the fuck off. The thing is though, it's true. I'm not even sinking so much as just adrift and lost, waiting to be dashed against the rocks.

I nod. "Yes. I've left Banks and Redford. As your broker, I'm recommending you leave your stock with them. They'll look after it well for you." God, this is so much harder than I thought it would be.

"Not like you would." He counters.

I look up and meet his gaze. He tilts his head to the side, focusing on me. "Giles, thank you. Thank you for everything. I consider myself so lucky to have had you as a client and even more fortunate to have had you as a friend, but I'm done. No one in this city will hire me. I can't help you no matter how much I might like to."

A slow smile pulls at his lips and I frown in confusion. "Ah, Georgia. So serious." He waves his hand through the air. "So you had a fight with Landon's wife." He bounces his eyebrows lavaciously and I roll my eyes. "But this means little to me."

I shake my head. "Giles, you don't understand. I have nowhere to manage your stock from, no firm."

He glances at the table, a conspirator smile pulling at his lips. "What if I had a firm?"

"What?"

He slaps his hands down on the table as a wide grin spreads across his face. "Let's start our own firm!" He actually bounces up and down in his seat like an over excited kid.

I pause for a moment and let his words sink in. "Like Angus and Landon?" I whisper.

He nods. "Yes."

"I'm still not ready."

He shrugs. "But you are out of options, so you had best get ready." God, he says it like it's so easy.

"My clients." I say, shaking my head. "They're contracted in for two years with Redford and Banks."

"Landon told me he's broken their agreements. They are free to leave if they wish." My eyes pop wide.

"Landon did that?" Why would he do that. That's millions in stocks and shares. Millions that his company has just lost.

A wry smile pulls at his lips. "Eh, love will make a man do crazy things. Poor Angus is probably pulling his hair out." I can't think about Landon right now. I can't think about what such a crazy gesture even means.

Giles slides the binder across the table and opens it in front of me. "Now I've already drawn up the figures and we're looking at office space on Thursday." This is crazy, completely insane, and yet his excitement is infectious. Didn't I always say I wanted be the CEO?

32

---

3 months later

ROBERTS AND CO. Finance and Investment has been up and running for just two weeks, but business is booming. Eva came to me as soon as we were ready to open our doors and pretty much demanded she be my assistant. Turned out she'd already handed in her notice, and she is the best assistant I've ever had, so I didn't really have much choice. I have Eva and four other brokers working for me. Giles is thrilled that his new venture is successful, and I'm the CEO. I made it. This was and still is my dream and for the first time in my life I'm content.

There's a knock on my office door and Eva pops her head in.

"Mr. Brown here for you G." I roll my eyes. I don't know how many times I have to tell her to call me Ms. Roberts in front of clients.

"Okay, send him in." I shuffle some papers on my desk, standing up and tidying them away into the filing cabinet. I hear the handle on the door click and glance in the direction of the doorway, a smile plastered on my face, though these days I find my smiles are genuine. These are my clients, and I like talking to them. I make them money and that speaks for itself. I don't have to prove anything to them or earn their respect. The name Georgia Roberts is fast becoming a name that people instantly respect and clients from some of the biggest companies in the city are flooding to our doors. Of course Giles tells me that he always had faith, and honestly I'm grateful to him for seeing something that I clearly couldn't.

When 'Mr. Brown' walks in, my breath seizes in my lungs and I can feel all the blood drain from my face before a flush creeps over my cheeks and my heart leaps into a sprint.

"Landon." I whisper. I'm going to kill Eva.

I stand there in the middle of my office, gaping like an idiot. It's not like I never thought I'd see him again, we live and work in the same city, but I just...I thought I'd be a little more prepared.

Over the course of your life you meet thousands of people, some are inconsequential while others leave a lasting mark. Landon scarred me to my very core. He was the guy I was willing to risk it all for, even if I didn't know why at the time. If I had to go back, I'd probably do it all again, not through choice, nothing was ever a choice with him. If I'm honest with myself, I fell for him. What I felt for him scared me and rather than place my faith in it, in him, I ran. I've always relied soley on myself, and my feelings for him weren't enough to over-ride a lifetime of self-preservation. But now here he is, in my office. And it's all flooding back in like a tidal wave. I remember everything. Every single thing that lead us to this exact point.

He closes the door behind him and stands with his back

pressed against it. Damn, I'd forgotten just how good he looks, especially in a suit. I've never met a man as beautiful as him and I don't think I ever will. He smooths a hand down the front of his black three-piece suit, complete with crisp white shirt and a royal blue tie. A small frown line mars his forehead and his full lips are pressed together in a firm line as those dark eyes pin me to the spot. That familiar pressure settles on my chest, making it hard to breathe. My body reacts to him as it always has.

"Georgia." His deep voice caresses my name and it's as if no time has passed at all, as though it were only yesterday that I was sprawled on that desk never wanting to let him go.

His eyes flick around my office and a small smile kicks up the corners of his lips. "Nice office."

"Uh, thanks." I say. I have no idea why he's here. I haven't seen him since that night at the club and we haven't spoken since that day in his office and I feel bad. I have ever since I left with no word. He's crossed my mind a lot in the past months, but I don't look backwards because what's the point? You can only ever keep putting one foot in front of the other until you get where you want to go. Landon... Landon was collateral damage, and so was the piece of me that I left behind when I walked out of his office door.

I take a step back and lean against the desk, gripping the edges of it. "You let my clients go." I say, because it's been bothering me ever since I found out. Why would he do that? From a business stand point it makes absolutely no sense.

He nods and unfastens his jacket. "Giles is a friend." He tilts his head slightly and his eyes flick to my lips very briefly. "*You're* a friend."

Oh god, I'm suffocating in guilt. "You didn't have to do that. I left you without even a goodbye."

He tilts his head back on a sigh. "I always knew you

would run, Georgia. I just hoped it wouldn't be over that. I asked you to trust me and you couldn't." He shrugs. "I could have come after you if I'd wanted to." But he didn't, even when I saw him in that club. He didn't say a word to me. I was sure he hated me at that point.

I nod. "So, why are you here now?"

"Because I want to."

I frown. "What?"

He takes two slow steps towards me until he's only a foot away. I can smell the scent of his aftershave and it smells so safe, so familiar.

"I'm here because now I want to come after you."

My eyebrows shoot up. "What? Why?"

"This is the reason why." He says, pulling an envelope from his inside jacket pocket and handing it to me. I keep my eyes fixed on him as I take it and remove a handful of papers. The first page is an agreement between Landon Banks and Isla Banks. Divorce papers. When I turn to the last page, there are two signatures, his and hers, the date beneath her signature is yesterday. He's divorced.

"So you finally did it." I say, putting the paper back in the envelope and sliding it back across the desk to him.

He nods as he picks it up. "Yes, and she won't be pressing charges against you anymore."

I tilt my head to the side. "What did you do?" That woman was determined to press charges, declining any settlements I've offered her, even for ridiculous sums of money. She wanted to see me pay for fucking her husband.

"I gave her what she wanted."

My eyes go wide and I find myself leaning forward, swaying away from the desk. "Landon! You gave her half of everything?" Surely not, he must be worth millions, tens of millions.

"Not everything." He says pointedly, looking me in the eye. My heart thuds painfully at those two words. He reaches out, tucking a stray strand of hair behind my ear and cupping my face, a soft smile on his lips. The second his skin touches mine it's as though the last three months never happened. I had forgotten what his touch felt like, the element of invincibility he can instill with a mere look, a simple touch, because he's Landon Banks. "Not this." He breathes against my lips before pressing them to mine. We've always had a spark between us, but this is more like an explosion of sensation as my body remembers him, the feel of his lips, the stroke of his tongue.

His hands cup my face and I wrap my fingers around his wrists, holding him close. He pulls away, leaving me breathless as he touches his forehead to mine. "So, Georgia Roberts, CEO...tell me, can a boss fuck another boss?"

"Is that you asking me on a date?" I smile.

He flashes me a cocky smirk. "A date? No. We both know you're already mine, kitten. I just want everyone else to know it too."

EPILOGUE

Two years later

"GOD, this shit never gets any more interesting." Landon whines, letting his head fall back so he's staring at the ceiling. I jab him in the ribs with my elbow and he grunts, sitting back up.

"Ow. So violent."

"Listen. You might learn something." I hiss. A couple of people near us throw annoyed glances our way but of course Landon doesn't give a shit.

The woman on the podium continues with her presentation on market trends and fashionable investment. I listen. Landon plays on his phone.

When the presentation is done, I stand up and leave with Landon in tow. He snakes an arm around my waist and I slap him away which I swear only makes him worse. There's a bar outside the amphitheatre where people talk in small groups. This is an ideal place to suss competition, and it's like a Who's Who of the business world. This event is invitation only, and I couldn't believe that I got an invite in only my second year of business, but the truth is, my firm turns over more money than some that have been doing it for ten times as long.

"Georgia." Someone says, clearing their throat behind me. I turn around and come face to face with Martin Collins. Well, sometimes fate smiles and I smile back because fuck, this is too perfect.

An awkward expression crosses his face as he looks up at Landon before quickly dropping his gaze again. "Banks." He says curtly. It reminds me of when a dog approaches an alpha, refusing to look it in the eye for fear of causing offence. Landon doesn't even acknowledge him.

"Collins. How are you?" I say, trying to play nice. He drags a hand through his overly Brill-creamed hair, tugging at the tie around his neck. He looks dishevelled and messy. Come to think of it I don't know how he convinces anyone to give him their money. Him and Landon are like night and day and I know who I'd give my money to.

"Good. I uh, I just wanted to congratulate you on the new firm." The new firm that stole three of his clients in the last month alone. He holds out his hand to me and Landon presses against my side. Oh, Jesus. People know we're together, but when it comes to business I don't like people to *know*. Obvious relationships are unprofessional.

I place a restraining hand around Landon's wrist, keeping it behind my back so Collins can't see while I shake his hand. "Well, thank you." I smile. He nods before disappearing.

"He looks at you like he wants to fuck you." Landon grumbles, his chest vibrating against my arm.

I turn my gaze to him and my eyes hone in on his lips. As we all know, I have problems following my own rules when it comes to him. "So do you."

He cocks a brow. "Ah, but you're mine." I just roll my eyes. We moved in with each other a couple of months ago when we bought an apartment just outside Mayfair. Behind the closed doors of our home, he owns me body and soul and he knows it, but out here... out here I'm the bitch that no one wants to pet. Honestly I think he likes it. The more of a bitch I am, the harder he fucks me when I get home.

"Lets go." He eyes me in that way of his and I know it's a command, not a request. I oblige, allowing him to keep his hand in the small of my back as he guides me to the lift.

As soon as the doors close he presses me against the wall and grabs my jaw roughly, forcing my head to the side. My breath hitches when he kisses up my neck before nipping at my earlobe. "Your arse looks incredible in that skirt." He growls against my ear. I press my hands against his stomach, feeling his muscles tense and flex through his shirt. I shiver as his breath washes over my neck and my skin breaks out in goose bumps. "I'm going to fuck it later." He promises. He releases his grip on my jaw and presses his lips against mine, swiping his tongue over my bottom lip. I rub my palm over his crotch, feeling his hard dick twitch against my hand.

"All yours." I breathe against his mouth, squeezing my thighs together at the thought.

The lift pings and we pull apart as the doors slide open. I drag a hand through my hair as I exit, fighting a smile as I watch Landon adjust himself, falling into step beside me. His lips are smeared with my lipstick, and a few businessmen in the lobby flash him looks of manly respect.

When we step outside the hotel the heat hits me instantly making me want to strip out of everything I'm wearing. Dubai is beautiful but it's hot as hell. The town car sits at the curb, the driver holding the back door open for us.

The air conditioning inside feels like a comparative paradise.

When Landon suggested coming to Dubai for a week I was dubious, of course he timed it with the conference and I couldn't really say no. Now he's taking me to a penthouse that he recently bought here after he sold his previous apartment. He didn't say it, but I guess Isla had been there with him. Not that I would have cared. Property is property. Who's been in it isn't really a factor.

The car rolls through the pristine streets of Dubai until we pull up outside a building on the edge of the city, by the ocean. The sky scraper seems to stretch into the sky like a blade, the silver windows reflecting the desert sun like a magnifying glass.

I open the door and step out, once again assaulted by the heat. Landon rounds the back of the car and takes my hand, leading me inside. "Good afternoon, Mr. Banks." The doorman says with a heavy Arabic accent.

"Jeff, how are you?"

"Good, Mr. Banks, I'm good. Thank you." We step into the lift and I eye Landon.

"His name's Jeff?" I ask incredulously.

He chuckles. "Well, he tells me I wont be able to pronounce it, so...Jeff."

The lift doors open straight into the penthouse. And it's spectacular. The entire thing is open plan with the glass walls that Landon likes so much showcasing a view that stretches to the horizon. Dubai is a city of glass with the sun illuminating everything like a beacon.

There's a kitchen to the left and a lounge and dining area in front of us. The second level juts out like a balcony hanging over the massive room. Adjacent to the sitting room are sliding doors set into the glass. I walk over and open them, stepping out onto a balcony that wraps around the side of the building. Patio furniture is scattered around the space, as well as a small bar and barbeque grill.

That view though. I can see the Burj Al Arab standing proud on its peninsula. Dubai stretches out beneath us on one side, and the turquoise ocean and white beach on the other. I grip the metal railing that lines the balcony, running my hands over the brushed steel.

"Do you like it?" Landon says, coming up behind me and scooping the hair off my neck. I don't think I ever really realised before this point just *how* rich Landon is. Dubai is one of the most expensive countries in the world and he's living at the top of it. His lips press against the side of my throat as his hands cover mine on the railing. I close my eyes, tilting my head to the side and allowing him more access.

"I love it." I turn around, wrapping my arms around his neck. "I love *you*." And it's true. Somewhere along the line he became a necessary part of me, something I didn't even know I needed, but I do. And from the moment he walked into my office declaring that he had given up half of everything for this, for me, for us...I think that was the moment I fell unequivocally in love with Landon Banks. His hands trail up my back and I hear the slow lowering of a zip. "How much?" He lifts a brow, that cocky smile making its way onto his beautiful face.

He dips down, grabbing the hem of my dress and pulling it all the way up my body before discarding it on one of the nearby sofas. "How much?" He repeats, his lips brushing over mine as his hands move over my body slowly, his fingertips eliciting tingles of sensation. The setting sun beats against my back, contrasting with the cool air that's billowing from inside the air conditioned penthouse.

"A lot." I admit, pressing my lips to his. He releases my bra with a deft flick of his wrist, nipping at my bottom lip as he throws it somewhere off to the side.

"Good." *Good? Really?*

He takes a step back and then that crazy bastard gets on one knee, pulling a box from his pocket. "Oh my god, what are you doing?" I blurt.

"Well, I got you naked because you're less of a bitch when you're naked." He grins.

"Oh my god." I cover my face with my hands.

"I love you too, kitten. Marry me." It's not even a question so much as an order, so very Landon.

He hasn't long been divorced for fucks sake! "Landon... you're being ridiculous."

He holds up a hand, silencing me. "This isn't complicated, Georgia. This is you and me. And outside these walls everyone else is the enemy, but we're allies, in everything. I will always have your back." He always knows just what to say. "I love you. It's just that simple." Black and white. This is black and white. Love doesn't have shades of grey, because you're in or you're out, there is no halfway house, no get out clause or rules. It just is.

"Okay."

He laughs and tips his head forward. "You're supposed to say yes."

I roll my eyes. "Fine. Yes. Now will you get up?"

He smiles wide as he gets up and opens the box, handing me the ring which is a monster sapphire, the stone a rich royal blue. I slide it on my finger, and it looks...right. Without warning he bends down, grabbing me and launching me over his shoulder.

"What are you doing now?" I shriek. He slaps my arse and I yelp.

"Fucking my fiancé's sweet arse like I promised." He goes back inside and starts walking up the stairs to the second level.

"Wow. So romantic."

He laughs. "You love it." I do. And I love him.

Landon Banks always has and always will be a force of nature to me. Some people walk into your life while others tear through it like an F5 tornado, ripping long buried foundations out of the ground and sending everything spinning in a vortex of such power that all you can do is stand back and watch. Well I'm watching, and I can't wait to see where Landon takes me next.

THE END

Thank you so much for reading Dirty Boss.

Are you looking for more taboo romance? How about a dark and messed up ménage? The Game is free in Kindle Unlimited and available HERE.

OTHER BOOKS BY LP LOVELL

Sign up to my newsletter and stay up to date with new releases:
Join the Mailing List

Dark Mafia Series:

Kiss of Death series

Collateral Series

Touch of Death Series

Wrong Series

Bad Series

Standalones

Super Dark and Fucked Up:

Absolution

The Pope

The Game

Gritty High School Romance:

No Prince

No Good

Taboo Erotic Romance:

Dirty Boss

Website: www.lplovell.co.uk

Facebook: https://www.facebook.com/lplovellauthor

Instagram: @lp_lovell

TikTok: @authorlplovell

Goodreads: https://www.goodreads.com/author/show/
7850247.LP_Lovell

Amazon: https://www.amazon.com/LP-Lovell/e/B00NDZ61PM

Printed in Great Britain
by Amazon

80518536R00132